# A Yorkie's Tale

# A Yorkie's Tale

● ● ●

## Lessons from a Life Well-Lived

David L Heaney

ISBN-13: 9781975991326
ISBN-10: 197599132X
Library of Congress Control Number: 2017913825
CreateSpace Independent Publishing Platform
North Charleston, South Carolina

You will see rare beasts, and have unique adventures.

—W.H. Auden

# CHAPTER 1

• • •

# Rattus Rattus

MAN AND MAMA were perplexed by the alarming amount of weight Niles had gained over the past several weeks. For a Yorkshire Terrier, even a small weight gain was obvious.

"I have him on that expensive food for older dogs," Mama called from the other room.

"Well, he looks fat, and I think you're probably feeding him too much of whatever he's eating." MAN laughed as he scooped up Niles. "Look at Mr. Jelly Belly!" he said, patting his round, hairless tummy. MAN sat in his big red leather chair and placed Niles next to him. "He's an active, old boy, so why else would he be gaining weight if you weren't feeding him too much?"

"I haven't changed a thing, so don't look at me!" Mama dismissed MAN's remarks as she headed into the bedroom to answer the ringing phone.

Niles found a peculiar sort of comfort in the predictability of his home's evening routines. Mama chatted quietly in conspiratorial tones with friends. Every so often, she would erupt in whoops of shrill laughter, startling Niles in spite of his poor hearing. But he understood this to mean she was happy and so, therefore, was he.

It was the lazy rhythm of the evening's rituals he liked especially well, with MAN stationed in his red leather chair, clutching his wine glass and watching *Jeopardy!* Geddes and Tamar, Niles's adopted siblings, lay like bookends at opposite ends of the couch. Tamar, a sleek and shiny black and brown Doberman, was all muscle, grace, and elegance. She exuded confidence, looking you straight in the eye with an earnest expression that was uncanny. Now, losing a battle to stave off sleep, she alternately furiously chewed the tennis ball she held in her mouth, then nodded off, chewed, then nodded off. At the

1

other end lay Geddes, a bronze-colored lab mix with haunting, yellow eyes and a rather anxious demeanor—perhaps a matter of breeding or some unknown trauma inflicted on him by his previous owners who had dropped him at the animal shelter when he was a puppy. He avoided eye contact to the extent possible and looked like a shamed child when human eyes locked on his. Still, he was a fine dog and a loyal friend.

Beyond his appreciation for predictability and these sorts of evenings, Niles didn't spend much time contemplating whether he was content. However, if you had asked him, in all likelihood, he would have told you that he would be truly content if you could find him something to eat. It had been less than an hour since he'd eaten, but time between meals was interminable. The truth was, Niles was *always* hungry. Besides, dinner was always a hurried affair, a race to finish every crumb in his bowl before Tamar finished hers and began lurking nearby, waiting for any opportunity to snatch what Niles thought of as a meager ration to begin with. So dinner was about moving food from bowl to mouth as quickly as possible and was little more than a memory within minutes.

Niles was not a terribly *serious* dog prone to reflection and deep thoughts. Rather, he was a cute dog, which he seemed to appreciate. In humans, he elicited a response similar to infants. He was small and cute. His appearance begged people to pick him up and coo, "Why, you're just the cutest little baby I've ever seen." Niles knew small and cute was good when you had to compete with a big sister and brother for a scrap tossed their way after dinner. So, he didn't mind being picked up, which people often did because he *was* so small and cute. This would have been impossible for Geddes because he was much too anxious, and Tamar, too big.

He was not one of those small dogs that projected vanity, with puffy poodle dos, or the long and silky cuts of Yorkie show dogs who looked like walking wigs. He was cute in a scruffy, rumpled sort of way, wearing his silky hair close-cropped in a sporty and masculine fashion. Mama was insistent that his silver and brown locks be cut shorter than most Yorkies except for a tousle of hair on top of his head that fell in his eyes and a moustache that covered his muzzle setting off a black button nose. His eyes were black and soulful with milky gray cataracts that betrayed his age. His voice, while generally hoarse, still had a childlike quality to it that captured both his sincerity and naiveté.

Mama and MAN rarely became angry with him as they did with Tamar and Geddes. Niles might leave a little poop in some discrete corner of the house that could go unnoticed for days. When finally discovered, MAN or Mama generally concluded it was too late to discipline him, invariably causing Geddes to shake his head in wonder at how easily MAN and Mama were manipulated. Finally, it should be pointed out that Niles was a practical dog who aimed to get along and had successfully done so for pretty much all of the ten years he had resided with Mama and MAN after they had adopted him from that dreary animal shelter.

On this particular evening the weather was warm, so the front door was open, allowing the three dogs to come and go into the fenced yard as they pleased. Niles padded down the steps, unnoticed, into the old home's walled front courtyard, followed the stones that marked the path to the backyard gate where he easily slipped between the wrought-iron bars and headed into the backyard. The backyard was small, as were most in the neighborhood. On each side, they shared a fence with a neighbor, and the fence along the back of the yard abutted an alley that ran along the backs of all the homes on their side of the street.

Niles's yard, like so many others, was planted with fruit trees—peach, fig, guava, and plum. Neither Niles nor his siblings were particularly interested in the fruit that would ripen and fall, often just rotting under the trees in the day-time sun. However, as luck would have it, the canopy of the neighbor's avocado tree cascaded over the wooden fence, displaying a bounty of avocados that hung on its boughs like ornaments on a Christmas tree. Niles felt quite differently about avocados, and so, when ripened avocados fell, it was like manna from heaven, allowing him to feast on the luscious, creamy, and fattening fruit.

The bliss he felt as he considered a never-ending supply of avocados enveloped Niles like a great bubble when a voice in the darkness interrupted his reverie.

That was when everything began to change.

His eyesight unreliable, he sniffed the ground near the fence.

"Well, well, well, I spy with my little dog with a big appetite," a somewhat high-pitched voice spoke from the darkness somewhere above Niles.

His ears pricked up, and he froze, listening for more. Nothing.

"Hello?" Niles called. Then he thought he had better be a little more assertive with whoever was trespassing. "Who is that?" Niles growled as he scanned the backyard.

It was a strain to see pretty much anything in the dimming light through his clouded eyes.

"I said, you look hungry," the voice called again, "but, you know, avocados are not especially good for dogs. Hey, pay attention, now! I'm *here*! Over *here*," the voice called, apparently noting that Niles was confused about where it was coming from. "Avocados are *very* fattening. Did you know that?"

4

At the ready, Niles stood tall, nose twitching. "What?! I'm warning you! Be careful, whoever you are. I . . . am . . . here. This is my yard, so you'd better show yourself."

He growled and waited, scanning the length of the back fence, looking for the source of this rude interruption.

"I know! I know!" the voice called. "Look up! I'm up here."

Niles moved closer to the wooden fence, looked up, and saw silhouetted against the newly moonlit sky the figure of. . . .

"A rat!"

He choked out these words and started coughing. Hacking, more accurately. It was an annoying flaw, he knew, and something of an embarrassment. For whatever reason, sudden excitement seemed to constrict his throat somehow, and he could do little more than bark out a raspy, dry, and regrettably ineffectual warning. He coughed a few more times and cleared his throat, making a terrible sound *ack, ack, agghhk!* that most thought was frankly quite distasteful. It was a display that even caused Mama and MAN to wince.

He tried again—

"A *rat!*"

Better. It was both declaration and accusation.

The rat shuddered.

"Easy there, my friend. It is true I *am* a rat. But not just any rat, as you seem to suggest. I am a *fruit* rat. Or, to be precise, in Latin, *Rattus rattus.*" He rolled the *r* in each "*rattus*," which was intended to convey an impressive level of sophistication that, unfortunately, was lost on Niles.

"What?" Niles asked incredulously.

"Humph," the rat grunted, equally incredulous. "A . . . *fruit* . . . rat. I'm not one of those garbage-picking rodents. You won't find me digging around in the trash." He pursed his mouth and wrinkled his nose as if having smelled something bad.

Niles feigned indifference and kept scanning the area under the avocado tree branches for any fallen fruit.

"No, don't confuse *me* with a common *trash* rat," said the rat, and here, he leaned down closer to Niles and opened his eyes wide as if to underscore this admonition. "I am a F–R–U–I–T R–A–T. . . . A *fruit* rat. I reside and enjoy my living far above the common trash rat. And, I will tell, you the perspective I possess is quite different from those whose greatest pleasure is to discover a moldy crust of bread or rancid piece of *meat* in some back alley garbage pail!"

They stared for a moment, taking the measure of one another. The rat, who was indeed an astute observer, could see that Niles was unimpressed. So, abandoning pretense, he sat back on his haunches and pointed his tiny left front paw at Niles. "*You* should have that looked at."

"What?" Niles responded defensively.

"That cough! It doesn't sound good. No, it doesn't sound at all good. In fact . . . and listen, my friend, I *do* say this out of concern . . . it is, well, unnerving! Don't take offense. Now, why did you spit out the word 'rat' as if it were a profanity? Please, let's not judge one another on stereotypes."

He leaned down from where he was perched on the wooden fence above Niles's head both to drive home the point he was now about to make and to allow Niles to see him more clearly.

"*Dogs* . . ." he began. "Before you put on airs, complaining about the habits of *rats*, let me just remind you that rats don't run around sniffing everyone's bottoms! I mean c'mon! What can you possibly say about that? It hardly puts *you* in a position to say rats are disgusting! Rats are . . . so misunderstood." He shook his head forlornly. "I mean, what do I do? I nibble an avocado here, an orange or a peach there. I keep myself clean and do my best to stay out of sight. Seems rather civilized to me. *Entirely* misunderstood, we rats are. But *dogs*!"

"Well, we have one thing in common," Niles interrupted. "I *like* avocados too. In fact, I like them a lot. And by the way, *rattus rattus,* I'm a. . . ." Niles, tossing his head back to get the hair out of his eyes, proudly proclaimed, "Yorkshire Terrier."

"Yes! Yes! A Yorkie!" The rat sat back on his haunches and clapped his front paws with delight. "How cute!"

"And you're a rat!" Niles fired back. "And rats are *not* cute!"

Honestly, Niles was being less than forthcoming on this count since the truth was, this rat was pretty cute. He simply felt it was inappropriate to be called 'cute' by a rat, so, as he sometimes regrettably did, he spoke before he thought. Stepping up as close as he could to the rat, he looked him over carefully. His fur was a handsome mix of charcoal, brown, and very light gray with a white chin and underbelly. His ears, almost translucent, were a soft pink as was his nose that twitched incessantly. The long whiskers and bulging, black eyes gave him a rather earnest demeanor. Niles didn't care for the long, dark, and hairless tail, but he bit his tongue, bearing in mind that negative remarks about one's appearance were personally hurtful.

"Tsk, tsk, tsk . . ." said the rat. "All right, all right . . . maybe not so cute." The rat leaned down toward Niles with an expression of sincere regret. "Let's try this again. I am a fruit rat, but I have a name." Then the rat bowed slightly and said rather formally, "How do you do? My *name* is Nathaniel."

"Yeah, okay. Nathaniel. I didn't really mean to say you didn't have any qualities that were . . . um . . . attractive. I suppose, for a rat—excuse me, a fruit rat—you're sort of cute. . . . I mean, you're fine."

Then embarrassed, Niles abandoned his feeble efforts to undo his unkind remark and quickly changed his tone to gruff again. "Nathaniel, huh? Nat the rat!" Niles said with great amusement, laughing at what he thought was a very clever remark. Then he thought, oh, he'd done it again; spoken before he'd thought.

"Ha *ha*! Very good! Very good!" Nathaniel laughed along with Niles, whose raucous laughter triggered another coughing fit, finally ending with that terrible *ack, ack, agghhk*! sound once again.

"Ugh." Nathaniel shuddered at the sound. "So, my new friend," he said, looking very pleased. "I am so glad to know you. You must tell me all about yourself."

Nathaniel sat back smiling, his pink nose twitching and his bulging, black eyes trained on Niles.

"Tell you about me?" Niles cocked his head, looking somewhat bewildered. "Tell you what? I don't know. My name is Niles. There's really not much more to tell you."

"Oh, nonsense, I'm sure there's lots to tell. C'mon, Yorkies are smart. You have a good home here. What do you do every day? I mean, what are you doing with your life, my friend?! What do you think about? You have a good story to tell, I'm sure!"

"Um." Niles paused and thought for a moment. "I like eating, I guess," he answered.

"Yeah. I know, I know. Me too. But what are you *doing with your life*?" Nathaniel insisted, pointing at Niles.

Niles shrugged as he tried to think of something clever to say.

"Eating. . . ." Nathaniel said. He sounded disappointed. He smiled and asked more sympathetically, "That's all?"

"Well, I am a simple dog leading a simple but comfortable life. What else can I tell you? I really like getting my ears scratched. . . . And, uh . . . I like to sleep. And, uh . . . I used to like to play ball, but it's hard with my new sister. She doesn't like to share much. So, really, what more is there to say?" Niles shrugged.

"So, that's it?" Nathaniel scratched his chin with his paw. "Oh, Niles, my boy." He looked at Niles sympathetically. "This is your life? This little yard? This little house? Eating and ear scratching. . . ?" Nathaniel shook his head.

Feeling somewhat ashamed, Niles said softly, "Yeah, I guess that's about it."

"Well, don't you find your spirit restless to see more, know more, broaden your horizons? Don't you wonder what's beyond the fences that surround you . . . that set the boundaries of this little place that has become your world?"

Somewhat sheepishly, Niles asked, "My spirit restless? What's that?"

Nathaniel patted his chest and explained, "Well, it's that thing inside you that gives you the urge to explore . . . to long for more! It causes us to be unsatisfatied with who we are and what we have. It drives us forward, inspires life's great ventures. It's our spirit that sends us on our life's quests. It drives us to become better creatures."

"But I *am* satisfied with what I have, with what I do. And I don't feel restless. Maybe I don't have a spirit."

"Oh, don't say that, Niles," Nathaniel pleaded. "I'm sure you do. I mean, I think everything has a spirit."

"Really? So what does it look like? Maybe I can look around and find a spirit if I don't have one."

"I'm not so sure that's how it works, but maybe. Or maybe it's sleeping," he laughed, "and we need to wake it up."

"Well, I haven't really thought about things this way before. I guess I really never thought of it at all. I mean, I have everything I need right here!" Then he added defiantly, "What's wrong with that?!"

Nathaniel, seeing he may have hurt Niles's feelings, was quick to respond. "Absolutely nothing! But, listen to me. How about we, you and me, Niles and Nathaniel, just have some fun?"

"Really?" Niles asked, standing up tall.

"No kidding! There's more to life than eating, sleeping, and ear scratching, Niles, my new buddy!"

"What are we gonna do?" Niles asked enthusiastically his ears now standing. Actually, only his left ear stood while the other remained in place, creating an asymmetrical aspect that only accentuated his bedraggled charm.

Just then, a voice sounded from the porch where a light had just been switched on. "Niles! Get in here! C'mon, let's go!"

Nathaniel leaned toward the sound to see if he could see who was on the porch. "Well, I guess time's up for you. But we are going to talk adventure, my friend!"

"Yeah, but we can talk . . . no rush. . . ."

Niles was enjoying their exchange and wanted to remain until he heard the faint but familiar sound of someone's hand rummaging through the biscuit tin. With that, he jumped to attention.

"Sorry," he said, "but it's cookie time, and well. . . ."

"No matter," Nathaniel laughed, thinking how dogs were such slaves to their cravings. "Go. Go get your cookie."

"Okay." Niles was already on his way to the back porch and now calling over his shoulder. "Glad to meet you, *Rattus rattus*. Or should I call you Nat?"

"Nathaniel . . . please!" he answered, but Niles was already up the stairs and the house door to the yard was closing.

Nathaniel made his way back to the top of the fence and reflected for a moment on the enthusiasm Niles showed for a mere cookie.

*I eat* when *I want*, though Nathaniel. *I eat what I want.*

He liked this and felt it gave him a sense of independence that allowed him to . . . what . . . follow his interests? He laughed at himself and leaped onto a branch of the avocado tree and made his way skyward. Higher he climbed, high above the fences that separated each family's home from the other. He found the wires that strung together a long line of telephone poles and created the path from yard to yard as far as the eye could see. He would walk the wire above the fence that protected people's privacy. The fruit trees were great, but up here, he saw so much. He might pause for a moment to watch someone grilling something fragrant at a late-night barbeque, or watch a dog wander about the yard, unaware of Nathaniel watching from above. Sometimes, he saw things he just didn't understand. Some of these were, quite honestly, confusing.

Everybody had their routine in MAN and Mama's house. Niles, Geddes, and Tamar liked routines. They knew what was coming and when. Food figured prominently into why all three dogs liked routines. During the morning routine, there was breakfast. Inevitably, there were some breakfast scraps that were apportioned according to their respective sizes. Niles wasn't fussy and was pleased to lick the dried oatmeal off the pot it was prepared in, crunch a cornflake or two, or even clean the yogurt bowl. Especially delightful were those days when the smell of sausage wafted down the hall to the bed where he napped. Among the three of them, he was probably best attuned to interpreting the culinary implications of the ring and clank made by certain pots, pans, bowls, and plates during breakfast preparation. Knowing how to read the subtle sounds of meal preparation allowed one to strategically position oneself for an extra treat like licking the bowl in which the eggs were scrambled or hanging around in the drop zone for a cornflake that might miss its target.

Tamar, still young and with her mind on other matters, concerned herself with things like retrieving the ball MAN would toss down the hallway. She patiently waited, holding her ball outside the glass box located in the bathroom where MAN and Mama stood under the rain, each after the other, without their clothes. After that, they would spend a great deal of time putting on clothing and looking into the glass above the place where the water ran, and they would spread the delicious, minty paste in their mouths. Geddes was a big fan of toothpaste and would stand beside MAN as he brushed his teeth, hoping MAN would share a bit of the foam in his mouth.

Niles had learned that there was little variation in daily routines, and a comfortable spot from which he had ready access to breakfast scraps was his only concern. The morning routine ended the same way most every day—a cookie, the admonition, "be good!" and the promise, "We'll be right back." Everybody knew they wouldn't be right back and that it would be hours that felt like weeks before they would return. But they did always return.

After the door closed, each dog usually made its way to the same comfortable spot where they would settle in for a good part of the day napping. Tamar liked to lie in the heat of the sun, so she would move according to where the sun shone on the carpet. On this particular morning, Niles followed Geddes back to the couch where he intended to sleep.

"Geddes?" Niles interrupted him as he was halfway up on the couch.

His two front legs on the couch and the back ones still on the floor, he turned his big bronze head, lazily fixing sleepy, yellow eyes on Niles.

"Um?" Geddes answered.

"Do you think we live a good life?" Niles asked sincerely.

"What kind of question is that?" Geddes snorted.

"I mean—we don't really *do* anything." Niles paused, sat back, and scratched his ear. When he finished, he turned again to Geddes. "I don't know. I guess I'm just wondering if we should be living our lives differently. You know what I mean?"

"I don't think about it, Niles," Geddes said a little impatiently.

"How about a spirit that makes you restless?" asked Niles, desperate to engage Geddes in conversation before he drifted off to sleep.

"A spirit? Who have you been talking to, Niles?"

"Uh, no one." He immediately regretted asking this last question, realizing he should have just let Geddes nap.

"I don't know anything about a spirit," said Geddes, "except that a lot of humans say we don't have these things . . . whatever they are. Again, Niles, I don't think about these things, nor do I think you should."

Settling in now, Geddes lay his head on the armrest of the couch.

"I just think there's a lot to see," said Niles, "and maybe there's more to living than this." He looked around at their surroundings to punctuate his point. "I mean, we do the same thing every day. Is this what life is about?" Niles sighed.

"Um hmm." Geddes' normally striking, yellow eyes were glazing over as he surrendered to his nap.

# CHAPTER 2

• • •

# A Dead Cat

"Geez, I'm hungry," Niles said aloud to no one in particular.

"You say the same thing every day, and you know we'll eat when MAN and Mama get home," Geddes griped. And then, as if by some miracle, the sound of the garage door could be heard opening.

"And that would be . . ." said Niles, "let me guess . . . Mama's car."

Niles laughed as he trotted over to the front door in anticipation of what was always a joyous reunion. And joyous it was, with wagging tails and excited barking, as if it had been weeks since Mama had left. Of course, according to routine, feeding followed her arrival, so the joy marking Mama's return spilled over into that which arose from the announcement of dinner. Soon after Mama arrived, so too did MAN, and again, the return home of someone believed to be long lost was celebrated.

Shortly after dinner, Niles lay on the couch, cozied up against Mama who scratched behind his ears as he drifted in and out of sleep. For all his restive questioning of Geddes, he was feeling that this was pretty close to perfect. But again, it was all he knew, so it was just another pleasant day melting into a lazy, moonlit evening.

Up until yesterday, Niles had always lived sort of moment to moment and never really considered one day better than another. Niles had always been pretty pragmatic, enjoying the pleasures that life brought his way and simply improvising when things were less than ideal. Cold and rainy days, for example, meant that he simply needed to sneak a "wee pee" in some discreet corner of the house in order to stay out of the wet weather. He was a practical Yorkshire terrier.

As he lay next to Mama, dozing—his mind gently moving from pleasant thought to pleasant thought—it stopped on a thought that occupied his mind quite often: food. He loved to eat, but dinner was over, and dusk was now settling over his world. But Niles was an imaginative dog, able to improvise. The image of an avocado found its way into his consciousness, causing his eyes to open with a start. One ear pricked up, and he jumped off the couch, casually slipping out the open front door. He followed the path to the right, hopped through the rungs of the side gate, and began nosing around in the gravel under the branches of the avocado tree.

The moment he hit the pea gravel, his nose to the ground, he sniffed and smelled for the fragrant scent of that precious emerald fruit.

"There's always something right . . . around . . . here," he half snorted, half growled as he rooted through the pea gravel that surrounded the picnic table under the avocado tree. "Nothing? There's gotta be something!" Perhaps intentionally, he complained loud enough to be heard.

"Nope, there's nothing!" Nathaniel said. He was perched on the fence top looking down at Niles some five feet below. "Nothing, that is, until your pal Nathaniel takes care of you, Niles. Right buddy?"

Nathaniel scrambled from the fence top to a branch where a very large and fine-looking avocado hung.

"Ah, my dear friend, Nathaniel!" Niles said, his mouth already starting to water.

"Bombs away!" said Nathaniel.

Nathaniel chomped down hard on the stem of the avocado, and it dropped only inches from Niles's head.

"Hey, watch it, Nathaniel! Night blindness! Can't see in the dark!"

The impact from the fall split the avocado open, and Niles plunged in, filling his mouth full with the treasured, green mush so that what Nathaniel heard after the reference to night blindness was mostly impolite lip-smacking.

"Night blindness?!" Nathaniel asked, surprised. But Nathaniel would soon come to understand that Niles was not a young man and that certain afflictions like the cataracts he bore as a gray, filmy lens on his eyes limited his vision.

"Yeah, it's not too bad," Niles lied, "and I don't make it a habit of sharing this information, so I would appreciate it . . . ."

"Enough said. I got it. Not a word!" Nathaniel drew his paw across his mouth to indicate his rat lips were sealed.

"So, I wanted to tell you that it has *been . . . a . . . day,*" Nathaniel said as he made his way down from the branch to the fence top, and then, defying what Niles believed were the laws of nature, walked vertically down the fence post in the corner.

Niles shook his head with amazement at this feat, barely looking up from his avocado. And then, dismissing his own observation, he said, " Hey, listen . . . this avocado is wonderful. . . . And . . . let me say thank you for your assistance." Then he took a deep breath and let it out very slowly. "I believe," he said, patting his stomach. "I believe I am full."

Niles sat down with legs apart, drawing both his own and Nathaniel's attention to the ample belly that now seemed to be pushing his haunches apart. Niles took another slow, deep breath and whistled a bit as he expelled it and smiled.

"Whew!" he said. "But that was good."

"That's some belly, my friend," said Nathaniel. "Better ease up on the avocados."

Niles patted his belly. Then, looking up at Nathaniel, he asked, "What did you mean when you said it has been a day?"

"I told you before, I *see* things."

"Like what?"

"Like *lots* of things. From up there." He pointed his nose toward the telephone wires that ran overhead. "I *see* more than you do from down here. Let's just say I'm a little worldlier, and well, honestly, I just *know* more than you!"

"Ha," Niles answered skeptically. "And what do you see that makes you so smart?"

"Well, I'll *tell* you what I saw. I saw humans dig a hole in their yard and put their cat in it!" Nathaniel crossed his arms, which now sat on his chest. "That's what I saw!"

"What in the world are you talking about, fruit rat?" Niles smiled, chiding his friend.

"Four of them. It was just. . . ." He looked over his shoulder toward the fence on one side of the yard and pointed toward the neighbor's, counting, "One, two, three yards over from here. I was minding my business when I spied from the wire the three of them standing around, watching the man dig a hole in the ground. I said to myself, 'Well, well, what's *this* all about?' So I watch for a moment, and the older child, a girl, is holding a pillow with both arms. The pillow, I can readily see, has something on it that is covered by a towel or some such thing."

"So what?" Niles sneered.

"So, they remove the towel on the pillow, and what do you think it was covering?"

"Don't know!"

"A *cat!*"

"*No!* What are they doing carrying a cat around on a pillow?" Niles asked with incredulity.

"Well, I don't know, Niles. Now listen, okay?"

Niles casually nodded agreement.

"So, it was a cat, C–A–T. Light tan and silver. . . . The cat does not move, so I figure he, she, whatever it is, has gotta be asleep. Right? Eyes closed. Sleeping, right? Are you with me here, Niles?"

"Uh-huh."

"So they take the cat off the pillow, and it doesn't so much as blink its eyes."

"Uh-huh."

""And they put him in the hole. . . ."

"Uh. . . ." Niles nodded, looking increasingly confused.

"And they cover him up with dirt!"

Nathaniel illustrated this whole exercise by pushing aside enough of the pea gravel to represent the hole, placing Niles's spent avocado pit in the hole, and covering it with gravel, creating a small mound.

"What? No way!"

"Really! I am telling you exactly what I saw. So what am *I* supposed to think?" Nathaniel shrugged his shoulders. "But wait! What was even stranger was this: As they were covering the cat with dirt, I could see they were *so sad*. The little girl's face was twisted, like she was in agony, and water fell from her eyes. Honestly, it was hard to watch, Niles. And then . . . and then. . . ." Nathaniel was becoming more agitated as he relayed the details of the story. "And then each of them except the boy took a small flower and placed it on top of the dirt that covered the cat and said, 'Goodbye, Deheune. We will miss you.' Isn't this the craziest thing you've ever heard, Niles? I don't know what to make of it. But I'm telling you, they were *upset*! What a strange sight that was, eh Niles? Can you imagine such a thing? I see things that you couldn't dream of."

He paused here a moment then turned his gaze to a bewildered Niles.

"You, my friend," said Nathaniel somewhat sorrowfully. "You have just this little world." He shook his head, gesturing to the yard. "And it's all you know. You don't even ask yourself what's on the other side of this fence. You are a nice dog yet so naïve. Indeed, unworldly! What kind of life is this? It's a big world 'out there,' Niles."

Then, squinting his eyes and scanning the horizon, Nathaniel spoke as if to himself.

"There are some curious things going on that are just begging to be explored," he said. Then, returning his focus to Niles, he asked, "How are you going to understand life if all you know is this tiny little world of yours?" Nathaniel rocked back on his haunches, his expressive front legs, like little arms, gestured plaintively.

Niles slowly shook his head back and forth, still looking down. "Well," he said, "that's weird, all right, but it just makes my head hurt. Why would you put a sleeping cat in a hole and bury it? And by the way, Nathaniel, just because you saw this very strange thing doesn't make you worldlier than me unless you *know what it means*! Do you understand what you saw? I mean, can you explain it?"

"All right. I do confess, my friend, I did not understand this highly unusual sight, but I saw it with my own two eyes!"

"If you did not *understand* what you saw, how does that make you world-lier than me? Seeing something does not necessarily mean you know or understand it!" Niles punctuated his statement with a few dramatic gestures like holding his paw up to halt the trajectory of Nathaniel's argument. He took some satisfaction in challenging Nathaniel.

Just then, a strange voice interrupted their conversation. "Lads . . . lads. . . . Stop. . . . That cat was dead."

The voice startled Niles. He crouched, shoulders raised and head lowered, ready to defend his territory.

"What!?" Niles barked. Turning around to face the sound, he straightened up to his full eleven inches and barked out a hoarse command for the owner of the voice to reveal himself. "I thought I smelled something," Niles growled.

"The cat . . . was . . . dead," a reedy, nasally voice with a peculiar accent spoke from somewhere under the succulents.

Nathaniel was already halfway up the fence when he looked back to see the silver snout of a beady-eyed possum emerge from beneath the jade tree. He stepped into the moonlight and grinned broadly at them both. He stood on his hind legs, holding onto a curved walking stick he leaned on. The possum, Nathaniel thought, looked somewhat like it might be a big, ugly cousin of his but with a coat of longer, course, gray and white fur. Nathaniel noted and admired the long, hairless tail, which rather elegantly curled at its end. He had a long muzzle, on the tip of which sat a soft, pink nose. His white face and black and pink ears were well lit by the moonlit sky.

This unanticipated and odd-looking creature just stood before them, grinning ear to ear, two rows of what looked to be very sharp teeth behind wet pink lips.

*Not the prettiest creature in the neighborhood,* Nathaniel thought matter-of-factly.

Niles, who now believed that he was indeed less worldly than Nathaniel and unaccustomed to novel creatures such as this, remained hypervigilant. The cataract in his left eye caused him to look further to the left of the possum in order to center him in his line of sight. Unable to make out the figure clearly in the dimming light, Niles felt it best to warn him off with a few barks and a growl, "Go on get out of here!"

The possum leaned toward the right to place himself in the center of Niles's vision. "I'm over here," he said, wagging his head and tapping his walking stick on the ground as if to coax Niles's sight directly on him.

"I *know* where you are, and I'm telling you, *stop*!" Niles coughed. "Stop moving. . . ."

Nathaniel winced, knowing the coughing would end in that terrible throat-clearing exercise.

Finally, *ack, ack, agghhk*, and the awful hacking and hawking, and Niles was done.

"Oh dear!" The possum put his front paws together and leaned toward Niles, conveying a sense of concern. When he saw that Niles was all right, he continued, "No, I was simply pointing out to you two lads . . . heh, heh, heh . . . that the cat, Deheune, was *dead*. And that the people you saw were simply doing . . . heh, heh, heh . . . what people do with their dead. Bury them and weep." He clapped his paws together, cleaning dust and dirt from them and accentuating the finality of the phrase. "Bury them and weep! That, my friends, is what the little girl was doing. Weeping! When humans are very sad, they weep something called tears. Most unusual, don't you think? And, crikey, mate have that cough looked at, or maybe . . . heh, heh, heh . . . *you* will be next."

Niles narrowed his eyes. Still uneasy, he said, "Hey, just hold on here a minute! Who *are* you, and what are you saying anyway?"

"Yeah! And what do you mean 'dead'?" Nathaniel asked, now back atop the fence.

"That's right," said Niles. "What do you know about this that Nathaniel doesn't know? He was *there*! Were you? And why do you keep laughing and grinning at us like that . . . heh, heh, heh?" Niles said, grinning back and mocking the possum.

And, as so often was true, as soon as Niles spoke the words, he regretted his tone. But fortunately, the possum seemed immune to the remark and moved forward until his face was very close to Niles's.

His eyes wide, the possum leaned on his walking stick and answered, "Oh, I'm generally *around* friend. Heh, heh. Yes, generally around." Then pulling back, the possum furrowed his brow and looked pensively at the evening sky. "And let's see now, what do I mean by 'dead'?" Again, he leaned in even closer this time to Niles. "Let's see if I can explain this a little better. Here's what I mean! I mean *this*!"

The possum's beady, black eyes rolled back into his head; he wobbled a bit, his walking stick falling to the ground, and then fell like a stone among the pebbles and dirt, raising a puff of dust that outlined the perimeter of the possum's figure, which now lay eerily still in the moonlit night.

Perplexed, Nathaniel and Niles stared at the possum, waiting to hear about *dead* or to see what he would do next, but nothing. He neither spoke nor moved, nor even seemed to breathe. Glassy-eyed and completely inanimate, the possum lay in the gravel and dirt—like an avocado, Niles thought.

Nathaniel and Niles looked at each other, but neither spoke. In tandem, they moved cautiously toward the possum. Nathaniel's whiskers twitched as he sniffed while Niles sneered and muttered a scratchy sort of low-pitched growl.

"This is quite odd. . . ." said Nathaniel. "Quite unusual. I don't much care for what he's doing, and I don't think this is good. In fact, I'd describe this little exercise as quite disturbing."

Niles snarled, fixing his good eye on the possum as he slowly circled behind him. Nathaniel inched still closer.

Suddenly, lifting his head, the possum spoke. "Leach!" he said.

Both Nathaniel and Niles leaped back from the possum, alarmed and in shock, watching this . . . this character as he leaped to his feet!

"The name is Leach," he said. "A possum, I am! I conduct my business . . . heh, heh, heh . . . during the evening hours." He raised himself on two legs, squinting and grinning, leaning on his walking stick, his snout close to Nathaniel's ear as if preparing to share a secret. He spoke slowly, accentuating each word. "And like you lads . . . I . . . see . . . plenty. I . . . heh, heh, heh . . . *know* plenty."

He made a dramatic pause. Now reflective, he bowed his head raising only his eyes to look at one, then the other.

"And what you just witnessed . . . heh, heh, heh. *That*, lads, is dead. A dead possum." Leach hesitated a moment as if distracted, then continued as if engaging in a second conversation with himself. "Well, not dead, *technically* speaking. Rather, I was <u>*playing*</u> possum . . . *playing* dead, as it were." He shrugged off the conversation he seemed to be having with himself and continued, "But that's what dead is like. Kind of like I was not there. . . . Odd, huh? Maybe it made you . . . heh, heh, heh . . . a little nervous, Niles?"

"Hey, how did you know my name? said Niles, still feeling uneasy about this stranger. "I didn't tell you!"

"I told you." Leach's grin widened, exposing glistening white teeth against a bright pink mouth. He pointed his walking stick at Niles and slowly enunciated each word. "I know . . . plenty."

"You weren't really sure what to make of it. It was . . . heh, heh, heh . . . confusing. It created uncertainty. One moment I was there, and the next." He cocked his head and looked up as if listening for something. "And the next, I'm still there, but, *not* there."

"You were *gone,* Mr. Leach." Nathaniel was quick to express his opinion on what he had seen. "All that was there was your body. I've never seen such a thing! But *you* were definitely gone."

"Yes, in a manner of *speaking,* I was gone. Now, know this, gentlemen. This is no ordinary feat. It's no fancy trick or game. I was *not pretending* . . . heh, heh. I was not *sleeping.* I was engaged in a, shall we say, *mysterious or, rather, mystical event.* A practice handed down from one generation to the next within the possum family. But, let me underscore lads that what you saw was not magic but mystery—a state of suspended animation, shall we say."

Nathaniel, who had been quietly taking this all in and seemed especially impressed said, "It was amazing, Mr. Leach."

"Saved my life a hundred times!" Leach quipped. "Dogs, cats, bears. . . . Ah, well, maybe not bears . . . heh, heh, heh. . . . But I'm telling you, being dead has saved my life. Heh, heh! You like that, gents? Being dead has saved my life! I *play* dead, and it stops someone even as big as that . . . heh, heh, heh . . . lovely sister of yours, Niles."

Niles growled a warning. "Watch it! I just might call her." He looked toward the house. He wondered how long he had been outdoors and why his sister and brother hadn't come out to pee. He still heard the TV and assumed everyone was content with dogs at either end of the couch.

"Doesn't matter," said Leach. "I *play* dead, and it stops 'em . . . *dead* in their tracks! Ha! You see, I'm just an empty package. And therein lies the mystery, my dear boys. It lies in the ability to make yourself . . . *empty*. When you free the force that animates your life, when you unleash your spirit to go exploring . . . heh, heh, heh. It scares the *hell* out of them! Hah!"

Leach smiled broadly and shook his head back and forth, chuckling.

"Scares the hell out of *every*body."

He remained silent for a few moments, both front paws positioned on his walking stick, seeming to look off beyond them.

"You see, lads," he continued, "I share with you, by means of this little demonstration, the dramatic impact that *even mimicking* death has on *all creatures*. Why? Heh, heh. . . . Did you ask why?"

Niles nodded agreement, his eyes wide and mouth agape.

"Because it's what's in*side* the package that matters most," said Leach, "that we relate to what's inside another. Heh, heh, heh. Who or what is interested in an empty package? Oh, dear, what a disappointment! A wadded up, empty bag of your favorite dog food. Awful! An *empty* box under the Christmas tree. Frightfully cruel! I ask you who is interested in that? But what you saw was more than a possum *playing* dead. This was no game. What you saw was a body without its spirit . . . without its soul. *Sans Spirit. Ex spiritus*, gents! *Expired*! To have the sort of impact to stop even the most powerful attacker in her tracks, you must be *empty*. . . . You must release your spirit to wander, apart from your body.

"But wait!" Niles asked clearly troubled. "How can you get your spirit back if you have let it go?"

Leach smiled broadly at Niles and said, "Sing it back home." Then Leach chuckled again and clapped together his front paws as if asking for their attention. He bowed his head and then lifting it looked at each of them intently for a moment. Then turning his paws so the palms faced up, he very softly sang:

*Send your spirit off to wander*
*Among the stars, the skies, and yonder.*
*Wisdom, insight, beauty gained,*
*Our world, our life, our vision aimed*
*Toward higher goals, a greater good*
*For those who, restless, think they could*
*Understand their life's call*
*And how it fits within it all*
*What difference, tell me, will I make*
*To those along the path I take*
*The purest truth is yours to own*
*But known by spirit and it alone.*
*Release and let its seeds be sown*
*But ne'er forget to sing it home*

Leach, whose eyes had been closed as he sung, slowly opened them and smiling warmly at Nathaniel and Niles. Leach then spoke. "A body without a spirit is . . . well, heh heh heh dead."

*Spirit,* Niles thought. Again, there was that word.

"Spirit," Leach says, makes us alive. "*En spiritus,* gentlemen. *Inspired!* To have spirit h. Think about it, lads. Isn't language lovely. Ha ha! And a body without a spirit is dead . . . *expired.*"

"I don't get it," Niles said. He looked at Leach and then to Nathaniel, puzzled.

"Yes, confusing old boy, I'll admit. Especially because there are so many creatures wandering about without their spirit. In a way you can be be alive but dead." Leach scratched his chin. "Hmmm. You are indeed quite correct in your assessment here, Niles. It is confusing! That we can say with some certainty." Leach looked at his audience and was not certain he was really getting through to them. "Oh, c'mon now, Niles lad," said Leach. "It's the spirit that puts the light in your eyes and love in your heart!"

"Well, that's all fine, Mr. Leach," Niles said sheepishly, "but I'm not sure I have a spirit. I mean, I'm not restless. I'm not inspired or expired. I'm just a Yorkie living my life with my brother, sister, Mama and MAN."

"Aye! Of course you have one! You're alive, aren't you, lad?" And then Leach added, "You *both* do. It's right there." He tapped his walking stick on Nathaniel's chest who put his paws over the place where Leach had touched him.

"Really?" both Nathaniel and Niles responded.

"Oh, yes! And don't you listen to anyone who tells you differently!"

Niles could see that this was a sensitive issue for Leach, as he began to pace back and forth as he spoke.

"Beware the gasbags, lads, who prattle on about what they don't know. There are many humans who do this with not the least bit of animal understanding." Leach paused a moment as if tending to some fleeting thought, then looked up at Niles and Nathaniel and continued. "Acting as if we animals were not in possession of a soul...a spirit... heh, heh . . . acting as if humans alone owned all things spiritual." Leach became quite passionate, raising and then lowering his voice, gesticulating this way and that to drive home his points. "Such arrogance! A dead animal in the road for which no one grieves?" Leach shook his head and seemed exasperated. "Why, the whole notion is absurd! And driven by ignorance. Heh, heh" Then, looking at Niles and Nathaniel, he smiled. "Ignorance informed by arrogance, lads, or maybe the other way around. Believe no one who tries to tell you that you lack a soul or that animals have no spirit." Leach stood all the way up on his back leg and jabbed his walking stick at the night sky to punctuate his conviction. "Your desire to know more—that which makes you hungry for friendship and love, that which compels you to open your mouth and speak, to question what others tell you is true—are all ample evidence that you are *inspired* indeed, my dear boys, and you should not forget it."

Both Nathaniel and Niles admired Leach's oratory skills and were awe-struck by the gravity of a subject that was entirely new to them. Leach paced for a moment in silence as he gave time for his words to sink in. Then he walked behind them and stood, placing a hand on each.

"Behold," he said. "My restless friends full of soul and spirit! Ha *ha*. Now come sit for a moment, while I have a word with you on some very important matters."

Niles and Nathaniel sat with their backs to the fence in the darkest part of the yard. Leach sat before them.

"Now," said Leach, "through practice, I have learned to allow my soul, my spirit, to wander while I remain in a state of . . . let's call it something like sleep only much deeper. But my spirit most reliably returns; and it always returns when I sing it home. So, lads, you have learned something very important this evening! Something you can practice. Remember . . . empty! But let me continue. *My* spirit rejoined my body, but the *cat*. . . . This is something quite different. That cat's spirit picked up and left and is not going to return to the cat. Or let me put it another way. Deheune is gone, and all that's left is a cat! You understand this, lads, yes? The cat that you saw was *really* dead. I mean gone . . . kaput . . . lights out. No more. Just a cat suit. Not coming back. Deheune, gone. . . . Cat left behind. Understand?"

Leach eyed the two of them.

"Um, I guess," said Niles. "But what does *that* have to do with us?" He was anxious that this may be perceived to be a naive question.

"It has *everything* to do with you . . . *and* you," Leach said, pushing his face up close to Nathaniel's. "Death comes to each one of us, lads. Empty package. It's when *you* leave the package. One day, *you* just get up and leave *it* behind like an old suit. Heh, heh, heh. . . . It's a fact of life! Get it? To die is a fact of life. Get used to it."

Leach dusted off his front paws and folded his arms against his chest. He raised his eyebrows and looked inquisitively at Nathaniel and Niles to gauge their reactions, all the while grinning that silly grin. Both stared wide-eyed and open-mouthed, looking at Leach and expecting him to say more.

Nathaniel swallowed hard and, while patting himself all over, said, "So, there's me. . . ." He pointed to his chest. "And then, there's another me? This is too hard for me to understand!"

"Everything that lives," Leach said slowly, "eventually dies. The part of me that . . . heh, heh, heh . . . laughs and cries, loves and hates. . . . The part of me that wants to explain this to you eventually abandons my body. Bodies grow old and tired and eventually wear out, but our spirit goes on forever. That's true for everything!"

Nathaniel stared for a moment in disbelief. Then, he croaked out, "You mean . . . me? You mean at some point *I* will leave *me*?" Nathaniel, listening to his own words, shook his head thinking the whole idea preposterous.

"Aye." Leach nodded casually. "And him." He nodded toward Niles.

"Oh yeah?" Niles said skeptically. "So here's a question I'd like you to answer. When *I* leave *me*, just where will I . . . *me* . . . go? You said the spirit may go wander, but how about when you're dead? Then what!? Where does it go when this happens? When you die?"

"*That*, lads. . . ." Leach held up a paw, pointing one of his tiny pink fingers skyward. "Is a mystery."

Niles's head began to hurt from all the strange things Leach was saying. "I don't know," he said. "This is too much for me to think about. I've never heard of these sorts of things. Maybe I'm hungry. An avocado might be nice about now." Niles seemed to be rambling as he looked around the yard. Then his eyes came back to Leach. "If all you do is die, then what's the point of. . . ?" His voice trailed off. "Maybe I'm thinking too much. But . . . maybe, Nathaniel, you're right, and my world *is* too small because I don't understand. And if I'm gonna die, then I need to . . . I don't know. Maybe I need to think more about how I should live, I suppose."

"Oh, you are a bright one, you are!" Leach nodded, smiling. "It's a fine idea to be asking yourself that question: Am I living the life I am supposed to be living? Heh . . . heh . . . heh. . . . You are a wise one, you are!"

"When will this happen to me?" Niles asked Leach.

"How should I know?" Leach seemed somewhat taken aback by the question.

"You *should* know, since you seem to be the one who knows all about this sort of thing!" Niles was both incredulous and annoyed. "I mean; why *don't* you know? Don't you *care*? Don't you *want* to know? I think it's important, don't you?"

"Aye!" said Leach. "It *is* important, but nobody knows *when*."

"Are you sure about this, Mr. Leach?" Niles asked skeptically.

"Yes, indeed, mate," Leach answered. "I *am* sure. That's precisely why it's so important to live well now!"

"So, you say we will all die, but you don't know when or what happens after we die?" Niles asked skeptically.

"Aye! *Seeing* dead doesn't mean you *understand* death. Seeing and understanding are very different matters, aren't they lads? You can see plenty, but . . . heh, heh . . . understand very little. Right, Nathaniel?" Leach grinned and winked at Nathaniel. "Seeing a dead cat doesn't mean you understand death. Sorry about that, mates."

Nathaniel grunted and looked at the ground.

"Oh," Niles groaned. "So . . . what am I supposed to do? What are *we* supposed to do? How do I know if I'm living the life I should be living? Who should I ask!? Am I supposed to do something important? Nathaniel tells me there's a big world out there, and all I know is this little yard here. Is there something wrong with that? Now you tell me that someday—but no one knows when, but sometime—I...me...Niles will be no longer."

"Ah, now hold on lad." Leach said shaking his head. "I didn't say Niles will be no more. The body which carried Niles around will no doubt grow weary and break down like all things do. But I am confident lad that the very thing that makes you Niles...". Leach said pressing his paw against Nile's heart. "That lad, doesn't wear out."

Niles pondered this thought for a moment then added, "Someday, I will die. I don't really know what that means, but it will happen. And I'll be gone, but my body will be here. Oh, this is too much!" Niles sat back and scratched his head with his back paw, muttering to himself. "I don't know *when* and I don't know *how*, and I don't know *what happens* after I die except what I *was* won't be what I *am*. . . . Oh, this is so crazy!" Then he stood up straight, cleared his throat as if he were about to announce something important, and said, "So . . . if we are going to die, *how should we live?*"

"Ahhh, that *is* the question!" Leach said, nodding his agreement.

"I want to live the life I'm supposed to be living," Niles said quietly. "But who's going to tell me when I'm doing that?" Again, he paused, and then his face brightened as if a brilliant idea had just occurred to him. "I think I know what I have to do!" He cocked his head, then proclaimed, "I think it's time to go out and meet the world. . . . let's find out what it means to live—I mean, really live." Niles let out a long and weary sigh.

"Alright!" said Nathaniel, punching the air. "That's the spirit, Niles old boy! Of course, you should know more! We both need to *see* more, experience more to *know* more. We've gotta see the world, buddy! Live, live, live!" Nathaniel again punching the air with his tiny paw.

Leach held up a paw saying, "Lads! Heh, heh, heh. . . . Easy mates. I'm not saying that you should—"

Nathaniel interrupted Leach and stood before Niles on his haunches, his little arms spread expansively. "Oh, Niles my friend, there's a lot to see out there. . . . If you want to find out *how* to live, we need to get out there and start living!" And then he dropped his voice low and spoke solemnly, saying, "We are going to embark on a quest to discover how to really live. I mean *really* live." Then he shouted, "Live, live, live!"

"*Yes!*" Niles jumped up excitedly. "Thank you, Mr. Leach!"

Leach was about to speak when the back porch light suddenly punctured the darkened yard and MAN's voice called, "Niles. C'mon! Time to come in. C'mon boy. Let's *go!*"

Niles's ears pricked up at the sound of MAN's voice. He began a brisk trot toward the porch. Then turning around to Nathaniel, he said, "Tomorrow night. I'll meet you here just before the sun goes down." As he headed toward the door, he turned to look back and shouted, "So, we'll begin our . . . what? Our *quest* then. We're gonna live . . . *really* live!"

All MAN heard was Niles barking excitedly on his way to the door, causing him to smile.

Leach moaned, shaking his head. "Oh dear! Live, live, live. Whatever do they mean? I fear there are some semantic ambiguities. Heh, heh. Are we talking about living it *up* or living life *meaningfully*? I wonder if they know. Heh, heh. . . . But I suppose there is no other way to find those answers than to go searching for them."

"Cheer up," Nathaniel said, interrupting Leach's thoughts. "We get it. No use hanging around here any longer. Time to get out and live."

"Get it? Heh, heh. Get it. . . . Heh, heh," Leach whispered quietly to himself with an anxious smile.

# CHAPTER 3

• • •

# Escape!

THAT EVENING, AFTER MAN had walked through the house turning out all the lights and had climbed into bed with Mama and fallen asleep, Geddes (whom Niles believed was asleep), lifted his head and stared for a moment at Niles.

"What!?" Niles asked defensively.

"Do you know what you're doing?" It was a rhetorical question, for no answer would have been right for Geddes, and he didn't betray even a hint of amusement. "You're not a kid, Niles."

"What are you talking about?" Tamar asked.

Geddes momentarily turned to Tamar. "Go to sleep."

"I know what I'm—" Niles started to say, then stopped. "I know. Good night, Geddes. Good night, Tamar."

"Good night," Tamar answered.

Geddes lay his head down and wearily sighed long, and deep, and very low.

The next morning, Mama let Niles and his sister out in the backyard to do their business as she always did. Niles went through the prescribed ritual of sniffing around for just the right place to go when he caught an unpleasant scent that he followed. A bird lay still beneath the large picture window of the house. Niles knew that the fetid scent was of decay.

When he nosed the bird, pushing its body forward, the head fell forward, limp and unsupported, which shocked Niles. He looked the bird over carefully. It was a small bird, a feathered coat in a marbleized pattern browns and grays along with black and white. The bird lay on its side. Its tiny, gnarled feet appeared as if they were looking for something to clutch. The bird's open eyes

were dull black and staring at . . . what? Niles pondered whether they were simply staring at nothing at all.

Niles nudged the bird with his nose causing it to rollover onto its back. The feathers, especially those on his belly and around his throat, were surprisingly soft. Niles looked up at the window and could see a wet splotch in which several down feathers were embedded. Mr. Leach had been right, he thought. A dead bird was of little interest. No longer animated by . . . by what? Whatever had been there before the bird hit that window was now gone. The bird was, as Mr. Leach suggested, an empty package. What happened to the thing that made this bird sing, fly, catch bugs, and make babies? Where did it go when he had hit the window? Niles wondered if the bird had dropped whatever it was below the window after he'd crashed. Indeed, he sniffed the ground below the window, but there seemed to be nothing he could detect. What had the bird lost?

*Life*, Niles thought. It was life that the bird had lost.

And indeed life *was* lost because no matter how hard he looked, Niles couldn't find it in that bird or anywhere around it.

*So, when something dies,* Niles contemplated, where *does life go . . . the force that animates them . . is it lost?*

He had many questions, but he didn't know with whom he might speak. He wondered if, after life was lost, it could be found again. He wondered if he found this bird's lost life, would he be able to use it? He wondered if the bird had lived well—had lived the life he was supposed to live. Or maybe the bird had just lived for a short time, then died, leaving things pretty much the same as he'd found them.

Niles thought he wanted more than this. He didn't want to lose his life. He wanted to *live his life,* the life he was *supposed* to live.

*Whatever that means,* he thought as he walked away from the bird, did his business, and sauntered over to the fence to plan his breakout.

Looking the fence up and down and from end to end, he wondered just how he was going to get beyond his own yard, which now looked so much smaller that it had before he and Nathaniel had decided it was time to get out and find out what living was all about.

He sniffed along the back fence over near the avocado tree. At the base of the fence, in the corner of the yard where the fence met the earth, he detected an unfamiliar scent and could see a little bit of light from beyond. He scratched at the dirt and began making a hole.

"Ha *ha!*" Niles exclaimed, delighted at how easy it was.

His front paws heaved the earth from the base of the fence between his back legs where a pile was growing larger by the moment. He saw more light coming from the other side—

"*Niles!* What are you doing!?"

Startled by MAN's voice, Niles saw now he had gotten carried away and was definitely in trouble. He turned around, nose covered in dirt, only to find himself swept up in MAN's arms, who spoke harshly.

"*Bad* boy!" said MAN. "*No* digging, Niles. *Bad* boy!"

He hated to be yelled at and so, hanging his head, the remorseful Yorkie trotted back inside, where he crawled up on the couch and took a nap. While

sleeping, he dreamed a most unusual dream. He saw what he imagined were the people with what he guessed was the cat Nathaniel had described to him earlier. He saw how the people were standing before a newly dug hole in the ground, just as Nathaniel had explained. The shovel was lying on the ground just a short distance from the hole.

Lying on a pillow looked to be the sleeping body of a silver cat, again, just as Nathaniel had said, although Nathaniel hadn't mentioned the cat's markings. Niles watched from the porch as they placed the cat into the hole. Then, the MAN said something to the boy and girl that was difficult to understand. He said, "I know you are sad, but Deheune now rests in peace."

*If the cat is resting, why should they bury it?* Niles wondered.

Just as he was considering how very odd this all was, he was startled by the gentle purr of a feminine voice softly speaking from behind him.

*"Niles."*

Startled, Niles let out a yelp and spun around to see the silver cat sitting in the open doorway of the room in which he was sleeping; she sat perfectly still except for her tail, which moved like a snake, weaving itself in and around her feet. She looked directly at Niles, slowly closing and then opening the most beautiful blue eyes Niles had ever seen.

*"I am Deheune,"* she purred. It was the oddest thing, for she communicated without speaking.

Deheune's stare was intense, the piercing blue eyes fixed on Niles, who heard a kind of melodic purr over which unspoken words found their way into Niles's thoughts.

*"That which you see is still really me.*
*I am Deheune for eternity.*
*I will be with you, and you with me.*
*So listen to my words, listen carefully.*
*The life you are seeking, of sunshine and bliss,*
*Will disappoint you because it's*
*Not this, not this."*

"Hey, Niles!"

Niles sat up straight, looking around.

"Are you okay?" said Mama. Sitting on the edge of the couch close to where Niles had been sleeping, she patted and scratched his head. "Poor little guy. You must have been dreaming!"

"Dogs don't dream," MAN called from the other room.

Niles leaped off the couch, shaking off the remnants of his nap. He'd never had such a dream before. Of course, he had chased cats in his dreams, but never had one spoken to him before. And such a strange thing she'd said.

34

*She*, he thought. *Yes, the cat was a she.*

He sat back on his haunches and scratched his ear, thinking it was all too complicated to worry about. He had other things on his mind. He whispered to himself, "I'm gonna find out just exactly what it means to live. That's what I'm gonna do."

Even as he whispered these words to himself, he wondered what they really meant.

Padding toward the front door, he suddenly stopped. A new thought occupied his mind. He was hungry. It must be time for dinner.

After dinner, MAN and Mama sat in their chairs, MAN watching *Jeopardy!* and Mama reading a book. Niles nuzzled up on the couch next to Mama and started to doze when he remembered his promise to meet Nathaniel in the backyard. No one took notice as he stood up, stretched, jumped from the couch, and quietly scooted out the door to the backyard.

"Nathaniel," Niles whispered in a kind of gravelly growl, searching for any sign of movement in the dimming light.

"Over here," Nathaniel called.

"Over where?!" Niles answered. "You know I can't see well at night!" He sniffed the ground and picked up Nathaniel's scent near the avocado tree.

"Here, I am," said Nathaniel. "That's it. Right here."

Niles found an avocado and stopped to enjoy it.

"What are you doing?" called Nathaniel. "C'mon, Niles. Everything's ready!"

"Ready?"

"Yeah, look." Nathaniel ran to the fence where he wriggled through a hole he had dug at the bottom. "C'mon!"

Still chewing, Niles moved close enough to see that Nathaniel was on the other side of the fence.

"You need to dig the hole a little wider," said Nathaniel.

Suddenly, Niles felt frightened. He started slowly digging, looking back at the house with the warm glow of light it cast on the yard.

"C'mon, Niles, dig!"

He looked at the hole and began digging furiously, throwing the dirt between his legs as he had earlier that day, and in no time, the hole was big enough for him to squeeze under the fence . . . which he did, after taking one final look at the house.

On the other side of the fence was an alley lined with fences of differing colors that belonged to other homes. Niles stared down the alley dimly lit by a streetlamp. The fences went on and on.

"Wow," Niles said softly.

Nathaniel extended his paw, gesturing up and down the alley, and whispered to Niles, "Behind every one of those fences there is a backyard different from yours."

"Wow," Niles again whispered as he stared down the alley.

"C'mon, let's get going, Niles," Nathaniel said.

They walked down the dimly lit alley, passing yard after yard. Every so often there were gaps in the wooden fences through which Niles peered to see what was happening. He saw the warm glow of each home's interior, people moving about and calling to one another from different rooms the way MAN and Mama did. He heard the familiar sound of a television playing *Jeopardy*, and he suddenly felt very sad. He had only been gone for a short while, but already was homesick.

He caught the scent of another dog and pressed up close to the gap in the fence when the stillness of the evening was shattered.

*Bark! Bark! Bark!*

A fierce-looking Pit Bull on the other side of the fence lunged at the gap in the fence through which Niles was peeking. Niles squealed, jumping back, his heart pounding wildly inside his chest.

"Who's out there?!" a man's voiced called from somewhere in the yard, but Niles and Nathaniel had quickly run ahead.

Niles was both afraid and homesick, and they had only been gone minutes.

*I've got to do this*, he thought. *Who wants to die without having ever really lived?*

So he steeled himself and together with his buddy Nathaniel, continued down the alley. They didn't speak but listened as they walked to the sound of distant dogs barking, an occasional cat's meow, and rustling in the trees above them. Niles wondered if the noise was from fruit rats.

At the end of the alley, they came to a street that Nathaniel explained they would need to cross. Cars occasionally zoomed back and forth, and they both knew this would be dangerous. Nathaniel was not used to streets and cars. He would have preferred the telephone and electrical wires or even a storm drain, but those were not options for Niles. So they watched and waited, and when it appeared there was a lull in the traffic, they jumped off the curb and ran for the other side as fast as they could. They had not counted on a car turning onto their street from a side street, and suddenly, it was bearing down on them with headlights like two horrible eyes. It roared by, barely missing them.

"Phew," Niles said, breathless. "That was a close call."

"Nah, we were fine—done it hundreds of times," Nathaniel lied, knowing it was better not to admit just how close a call that had been, for fear of shaking Niles's confidence in him. "I know a great place where we can camp tonight."

"Camp?" asked Niles.

"Yeah, sleep under the stars and all that sort of thing."

"Oh. . . . Well, I usually sleep on the bed with MAN and Mama. Will there be a bed for me where we're going?"

"Uh, sure there'll be a bed for you," Nathaniel answered.

"And will we have something to eat before bed?"

"Um . . . yeah, I'm pretty sure we'll have something to eat. Sure."

Niles was pleased to know he'd have a bed and a snack before bedtime and so fell in line behind Nathaniel as they hiked along the street. Nathaniel was racking his brain, trying to remember whether there were any avocado trees on the way to their camp.

After walking for a while, the number of houses grew fewer and fewer, and the paved road ended. The moon lit the gravel road ahead. Nathaniel knew that the house before them was the last one before they entered a small canyon where he planned for them to stay.

"Wait here," he told Niles.

He scurried up the gravel driveway, climbed the fence and jumped onto a tree, up the branches, and onto the wires that ran along the back of the home.

"Hmm, no avocados," he said to himself as he scouted the yard.

However, he did spy a garbage can with a lid that was not sealed tightly, so back down the tree and over to the side of the house he went, where he found the garbage can. He sat up on his haunches and sniffed.

"Definitely something to eat in there," he said as he climbed his way into the pitch dark garbage can. "Let's see," he said as he sorted through the contents. "Coffee grounds, no. Lettuce, no." However, he did take a moment to enjoy some of the wilted lettuce himself. "Uh, what's this? A hamburger! Perfect!"

He dragged the partially eaten hamburger out of the can and down the driveway where he found Niles exactly where he had asked him to wait.

"Voila!" Nathaniel exclaimed and presented Niles with the half-eaten burger and soggy bun with the tell-tale yellow and red smear of mustard and ketchup, some of which was smeared all over Nathaniel's side.

Niles devoured the burger, or rather what was left of it. "Where did you find such a delicious hamburger way out here?" he inquired.

"Oh, I stashed one away for you earlier," said Nathaniel. He had the mistaken notion that Niles would have been disturbed to know it was from a neighbor's garbage can. The truth was, Niles was an accomplished garbage picker and wouldn't have been the least bit bothered to learn that Nathaniel had found it in some stranger's trash.

"Well, thank you for that. I guess we're really starting to live now, huh?"

"Ha! Not yet. You've hardly seen anything." And with that, they followed the road to its end, where a dirt trail began with grass on either side as tall as Niles.

The darkness of evening surrounded them except for the light cast by the moon. Surely by now, Niles thought, MAN and mama would be wondering where he was. He knew they would see the hole he'd dug to get under the fence and would be very unhappy. He tried not to think about it and asked Nathaniel if he ever got in trouble for misbehaving.

"Are you kidding?" Nathaniel stopped and faced Niles. Then, leaning back so as to free his front paws, he pointed to himself and said, "No one tells me what I can and can't do. I am a free rat. A free being." Returning to all fours, they resumed walking. He smiled and eyed Niles. Then he said, "And that, my dear boy, is what life's all about."

Just as he finished saying the word "about," both felt a rush of wind and a frantic flapping noise. In the sudden chaos and commotion, Niles, who could barely see during the day, much less at night, looked over his shoulder and was startled and frightened by what seemed to be a huge, black shadow descending from the sky.

"Owl!" screamed Nathaniel. "*Run!*"

As Niles turned to look, all he could see was a great dark shadow descending on them both with lightning speed. The owl came in talons first and wrapped them around Nathaniel's entire body. Nathaniel was driven to the ground with enough force to knock the wind out of him. Nathaniel's mouth opened, and he let out a terrible shrill scream that only served to intensify Niles's instinctive reaction.

The look of desperation on Nathaniel's face filled Niles with an intense determination to save his friend. He spun around and with remarkable speed and grabbed one of the owl's legs, biting down as hard as he could. The owl's ear piercing screech heightened the sense of chaos. The owl thrashed about wildly, flapping his great wings while Niles refused to let go; he shook the owl by the leg who shrieked, "You don't understand!"

With his teeth clamped onto the owl's leg, Niles shook his head wildly, forcing the owl to release Nathaniel in a flurry of spit, blood, and feathers. Niles growled with such ferocity that Nathaniel's eyes grew wide, for he had never imagined Niles capable of such strength and bravery. Niles let go of the owl and kept barking and yelping until he coughed and hacked.

The owl escaped in an explosion of screeching and feathers, calling out as it flew off, "I . . . have . . . children!" But by the time they heard the call, the owl was no longer in sight.

Nathaniel's mouth hung open as he worked to catch his breath alongside Niles, who was clearing his throat after his coughing fit and shaking off the feathers that lay everywhere.

"Oh. . . . Oh, dear." Nathaniel, gasping for breath, spoke again, heaving for air between each word. "You saved my life, Niles." he paused and shook his head in disbelief over what had just happened. "You saved my life."

"Did you hear what he said?" Niles asked, his voice scratchy.

Nathaniel, still winded, shook his head.

"He said I didn't understand," said Niles. "And, when he flew off, he said, 'I have children.' Weird, huh?"

"Terrifying!" Nathaniel answered.

Niles laughed. "I'll say! There we were, the three of us all trying to do what we thought was right." He paused, realizing his remark had perhaps been insensitive, considering how close Nathaniel had been to becoming dinner for a bunch of baby owls. Niles quickly added, "Anyway, it feels like a complicated world, does'nt it? I mean, what was good for that owl wasn't so good for you and me."

"Complicated or not, the only concern on my mind at the moment is to thank you for saving this grateful rat." Nathaniel saw that Niles had blood on his muzzle from the owl's leg. He spat in his paw and went over to Niles and tried unsuccessfully to wipe the blood away. Then he said, "Thank you, my friend."

"You're welcome, my friend," said Niles. "Anyway, I'd much rather have you as a friend than a meal." And they both laughed.

They hurried the rest of the way up the trail to a place where a tree had fallen. Here, they followed the length of the fallen tree to the end, where a rotting stump sat. At the base was a small, hollowed-out section just big enough for Niles to curl up.

"Here's where we spend the night," Nathaniel said. He gestured to the hollowed-out portion at the base of the rotting stump. "But wait just a moment while I . . . just wait here."

Nathaniel went off into the grass that was much taller than him and came back shortly with a bunch of grass he used to line the bottom of the hollow, transforming it into a very comfortable bed indeed. Niles, who was exhausted, curled up inside the hollow, and just before he surrendered to exhaustion, he said, "I think we should call this Close Call Canyon." He laughed quietly.

Moments passed and soon Nathaniel heard the rhythmic breathing of Niles sleeping. Nathaniel realized that he, too, must have been wounded in the exchange. His back felt like it was on fire. He thought for a moment about the close call with the owl and what a good friend Niles was.

"Close Call Canyon," he whispered, adding, "I'll say!" and curled up close to Niles and soon also was asleep.

The evening was cool, and Nathaniel and Niles slept soundly. As Niles slept, the image of the people in the backyard come to bury their dead cat appeared to him once again. He watched as they stood in the backyard, holding the pillow with something clearly on it covered by a towel or maybe a large linen napkin. Removing the cloth, he saw the silver point Siamese cat that appeared to be sleeping. But the cat—as Leach had explained—was dead. The cat was there, but Deheune was not. That was how he had put it.

In his dream, Niles noticed that the people appeared to be a family. There was a MAN and a mama, and a young boy and a still younger girl. What he noticed in this dream was how very sad they all were. They were crying even as they laid the cat's body in the ground. As he watched the family, he heard a soft, feminine purr call his voice again.

*"Niles. . . . Niles. . . ."*

It seemed to him the very same silver point Siamese cat. She sat on the tree stump, her tail again slithering about and winding around her feet as if it were a snake with a mind of its own. Again, Niles was struck by the sheer beauty of her big, blue eyes, which she opened and closed very slowly. He found himself unable to take his eyes off hers.

She purred again, *"Niles, I am Deheune."*

> *"Selflessly, you fought for the life of your friend.*
> *Hungry to live now, and eager to spend.*
> *Your time and your effort to accomplish this end.*
> *Stay true to your quest now, but these words ne'er dismiss.*
> *The life you were meant for is*
> *Not this, not this."*

As before, there was something odd about the way she spoke, or rather, conveyed, these words because she did not actually speak them. Perhaps they were thoughts, almost melodic, very pleasant and soothing. Niles's attention was fixed on Deheune, who closed and slowly opened her magnificent eyes, never taking them off Niles until she melted into the stream of images that passed through Niles's mind as he slept with his friend Nathaniel by his side.

And as they slept, the moon sat low in the evening sky, eventually leaving the canyon in total darkness. In the darkness, a lone creature wandered up the path into Close Call Canyon and made his way to the hollowed out stump where Niles and Nathaniel slept. Leach had come to check on them. He saw them huddled together, cozy and warm, and smiled.

He looked around their camp to see that they were poorly prepared for their journey and shook his head. No food, no one keeping watch for predators. He saw from the great many feathers spread by the trunk that there had been some sort of incident. He looked more carefully at them both and saw the wounds on Nathaniel's back. Again, he shook his head and wandered about the area, picking leaves from plants here, and there a little bit of bark. He set these on a rock and, with a smaller rock, pounded them into a pulp and slathered it on Nathaniel's wounds while he slept. Then, gathering up the feathers along with some more grass, he covered Niles and Nathaniel as best he could.

After taking one more look around, he shook his head again, grabbed his walking stick, and muttered, "Be careful, lads."

He chuckled softly and made his way back down the path to return home, snacking on a few tasty snails he found along the way.

# CHAPTER 4

• • •

# Poppy

NATHANIEL OPENED ONE eye just as the sun started to rise to see what all the squawking and chatter was about. It was, as he anticipated, the noisiest group of birds he had ever encountered.

"What is all that noise?" Niles complained in a hoarse and sleepy voice.

"They're parrots," answered Nathaniel. He stood and brushed off some grass and feathers, then giggled. "Hey, what's with all the feathers? Ha! Look at you! You look more like a chicken than a Yorkie."

Nathaniel took a deep breath and blew as hard as he could. The feathers rose like a cloud above Niles, who stood and gave himself a vigorous shake, sending the grass and remaining feathers flying.

"Parrots?" Niles asked. "I don't see any parrots."

"Well, maybe not, but you hear them, don't you?"

Nathaniel was right about this. The parrots all spoke at once. And when one would get louder, they all would get louder, as if they were all talking over each other.

"They're up in those palms and eucalyptus trees, and they blend in with the trees so they're hard to see. They have lived in this area for a long time. There is a story that long ago, some humans kept a couple of them as pets in a cage. The legend is that one day, a gigantic parrot the size of an eagle opened the door to their cage, allowing them to escape and, well . . . here they are. Only now, there must be hundreds!"

"It sounds like it! Why do you think they left their cage, Nathaniel? Were they unhappy?"

43

"I don't know," he answered. "Probably wanted to find out how to live the life they were meant to live!" He laughed. "It's not just you and me who are on this journey, Niles."

"Yeah, maybe," Niles laughed too. And then, without any warning, the parrots all at once took flight in a chaotic commotion of flapping wings, squawking and screeching. "Wow. There they go."

Niles saw them scatter across the sky—green and red and yellow and orange,—then organize themselves with the precision of high-flying geese and fly off together, all in the same direction to who knew where.

"I wonder where they are going," Niles said, still looking at the sky where the parrots quickly disappeared from his limited view.

"They're off in search of, uh . . . lost treasure," said someone behind them. It sounded like the voice of a young girl.

Niles spun around to see that one of the parrots remained behind and was perched on a stump no more than a few feet from where he stood.

"Oh!" Niles said, looking at her with wide eyes. "Lost treasure?"

"Nah! Don't be so gullible," she laughed. "They're just looking for another tree where they can eat and chat!"

"Oh," Niles answered, downcast.

"Eat, eat, eat. All day every day. It's all we do. It's *boring*!" she screeched.

"Okay, we get it," Nathaniel said. He had turned his head one way and then the other, his eyes finally landing on the chatty parrot, then added, "Honestly, I don't know when you have time to eat when you never stop talking. Blah, blah, blah, blah." He held up one of his paws and clapped it open and closed to mimic the chattering birds.

"Hmm. Fair point," she said. "But, where was I? Eat and talk. It's all they do, all day, *every* day. So shallow." She shook her head to accentuate her disappointment. "There are certainly more important things we could be pursuing in life than eating and idle gossip! Now, on to introductions." She looked at Niles. "And who are you? What are you doing here in the canyon? I don't think unleashed dogs belong here." She turned to Nathaniel. "And you? Are you really a rat palling around with a dog? This is an odd pair if I ever saw one."

The parrot chattered on and on, never seeming to take a breath, jumping from one topic to the next. Niles and Nathaniel looked at one another and rolled their eyes as she kept chattering. Niles was struck by how beautiful she was—a rich green coat of feathers with red and a kind of red mask that ran across the top of her head, encircling her eyes. There were touches of yellow along the edges of her wings.

"Well?" she asked impatiently. Again, "Well? What are you staring at, little dog?"

Niles hardly heard a word she said, distracted by her colorful apparel. "Oh," he answered, shaking his head to exit his rapture. "I was just admiring your beautiful colors."

"Oh!" The parrot seemed for the first time a bit surprised and self-conscious but then fluffed up her feathers as if to better display her colorful raiment.

"I thought dogs couldn't see in color!" she commented suspiciously.

Niles smiled and said, "I don't ever recall anyone asking me that question. I think I have a pretty good eye for color."

Niles studied the parrot for a moment, thinking she seemed rather bossy for someone who sounded so young.

"You sure like to talk!" Nathaniel teased with a smile. "I have never heard so many birds chattering at one time. How in the world can you call that a conversation? And, like I said, with all that squawking, when do you find a moment to eat?"

Nathaniel and Niles laughed.

"*They* love to talk," said the parrot. "I'm a lot less chatty than the rest of them. I am more the 'down to business type'. Really, I am. But I do have to tell you that we were talking this morning about one of the girls' dreadful plumage and how downright arrogant one of the boys had become since he molted.

Typical male. Thinks he's a lovebird, but he's just a conure like the rest of us. I know my plumage is beautiful, but I don't need to go around telling everyone that! And . . . uh, what were we talking about? Oh yes, we were talking about talking. So, as you can clearly tell, I don't just talk for the sake of talking!"

Nathaniel rolled his eyes and leaned close to Niles, whispering, "Gossip."

"Gossip? Call it gossip if you like, but how else are you going to learn anything? I learn a lot from talking with others. It's a big and complicated world, and believe me when I tell you that I've learned a lot in my travels, and I'm no shrinking violet when it comes to meeting others or pursuing adventures. You *can't* be if you want to learn anything!" Then she stood up straight and stretched out her right leg and right wing, then did the same thing on the other side, as if to underscore her last point. Then she leaned forward. "So, there we are. Now, my name is Poppy. And you are?"

"Happy to meet you, Poppy. I'm Niles."

"And I'm Nathaniel."

Poppy wildly fluttered and flapped her wings without warning sending a flurry of down into the air and alarming both Niles and Nathaniel who quickly stepped back. Poppy's many unusual movements were foreign to Niles and Nathaniel, but they were courteous and did their best not to act shocked when she exhibited little tongue wags or made odd head movements or fluffed up like a green puffball.

"Niles!?" Poppy cocked her head in that inquisitive manner once again.

"That's right," Niles answered.

"So *you* must be the one they were looking for last night."

"Huh?" Niles was puzzled as he looked at Poppy. Nathaniel winced, as he anticipated what was coming next.

"There were people calling the name Niles not far from here last night," said Poppy. "Walking up and down the street. 'Niles! Niles!' they called over and over. So, they must have been looking for you! Am I correct? Was it you they were looking for? And oh, by the way, they seemed worried. Very worried. Were you the one that they were worried about? And why would you do that? Are you lost, Niles?"

Niles hung his head, ashamed to have hurt MAN and Mama.

"They were worried?" Niles asked sheepishly and then added, still looking down at his paws. "I'm not lost."

"You don't act as if you are lost. But if you asked me if they were worried, I am telling you yes, they *were* worried. Oh, yes indeed! I imagine they still *are* worried. We all heard them calling up and down the street last night. 'Niles?' they called. Sometimes, they sounded a little impatient, like perhaps they were angry with you."

"Niles and I . . . well, see we're on kind of a mission," Nathaniel said somewhat sheepishly.

"Yes," said Niles. "Nathaniel and I are on a very important mission . . . a quest, you might say. I'm really not sure *what* to call it." Niles added, frustrated with the confused response they were providing Poppy. "You see, we have learned that life doesn't last forever, and then you become dead, and then they put you in the dirt, and then what do you have? Nothing, right? We want to learn how to live. I mean really live! Right, Nathaniel?"

"Yep. That's right. Yep," Nathaniel said confidently.

"And besides. I *will* go home after I learn what it means to really live."

Poppy flew from her perch on the stump and now stood before Niles and Nathaniel. She stared at Niles in silence for a moment, which made Niles kind of uncomfortable. But she was close enough to Niles that he could see she wasn't really looking at his eyes but appeared to be looking at the dog tag hanging from his collar.

"What?" Niles asked as he backed away cautiously.

Poppy stared, seemingly mesmerized by Niles's dog tag. And then, to Niles and Nathaniel's astonishment, she started pecking at the tag.

"Hey! Wait! What are you doing?" Niles said, backing away as she followed and pecked at the dog tag. "Stop!" Niles barked.

"Oh, sorry," said Poppy. "I just love shiny things. They're kind of magical, aren't they?"

Niles and Nathaniel looked at each other and shrugged. Nathaniel said, "If you say so, Poppy."

"Indeed, I *do* say so," she said, closing the subject. "Now, we were talking about those poor people looking for you Niles. And you were talking about a quest, not living forever and wanting to discover what it means to really live. Have I got that right?"

They nodded.

"So, how are you two going to learn anything down here in the canyon!?" Poppy challenged.

"Nathaniel here is able to climb up trees and into the wires high above everything else where he can see what might be the best direction for us to follow," Niles explained. "From way up there, I think he has a pretty good feel for where things are," he added a bit smugly.

"I see," Poppy answered. "Way up there, huh?"

Poppy flapped her wings and and up, up up she went in what seemed an instant. Up, up, up, she flew until she disappeared from Niles's sight. Then, as the two searched the sky for her, she reappeared flying so fast towards them that they barely had time to duck when she swooped in low, just over their heads, finally coming to land on the stump again.

"So," said Poppy, "you think Nathaniel's got the best vantage point for seeing just where things are?" She stared for a moment at the two of them. "Believe me when I tell you that I see things that neither of you can see."

"Okay, okay, I get it," Niles laughed. He lifted a paw, about to make a point. "But, let's be clear that just seeing something doesn't always mean you *understand* it," he said echoing Leach's words.

"True, true, true," Poppy conceded. "But there's really so much for you to know, and it's impossible for you to know what you *need* to know when your world is no bigger than this canyon—or no bigger than this small neighborhood here? I'll bet that Nathaniel here hasn't been any further than a hundred yards from where you two met."

Niles looked at Nathaniel, his mouth wide open. Nathaniel narrowed his eyes and pursed his lips at Poppy.

"No, wait, let me correct myself," Poppy quickly tried to amend her offensive (but true) statement. "I mean; most fruit rats are content to forage among the trees near their homes. There are, however, certainly brave adventurers among the fruit rats who have a great deal of experience with strange places and foreign lands."

Nathaniel rolled his eyes and said, "Okay, Poppy, knock it off!"

Poppy smiled, then continued. "I fly above all this and have a very unique view on things. I see things and know things that you could hardly imagine."

Nathaniel looked at Poppy thoughtfully. "You have a good point," he said. "Niles's world was only as big as his backyard. Certainly, my world is much bigger because I walk the wires and climb trees where I can see and know things that he can't. But you. . . ." He scratched his chin with his paw and gestured to the sky. "You . . . way up there, where you can see everything!" And then he asked almost desperately, "Do you know what it means to really live? Not just live but *really* live? To live the life, you are *supposed* to live? Life can be short, Poppy! We know this, and it makes living the life we are supposed to live all the more important."

"Well, I told you that I know plenty," said Poppy, "but honestly, I believe some of this to be utter nonsense. Let's call it, 'confused thinking'. What do you mean we don't live forever and then we die and are put in the dirt? It's gibberish, if you ask me."

"I know, I know," said Niles. "My head starts to hurt whenever I think about it. But Mr. Leach explained to us what happened to a cat Nathaniel saw that was there but wasn't there. He said the cat was dead. So even though the cat was there . . . I mean, Nathaniel saw him . . . he really wasn't there any longer. No purring, no meow, no hissing, no chasing rats." He gave Nathaniel a friendly bump when he said this.

"*Whaaaat?*" she squawked.

"It's hard to explain, Poppy," Nathaniel said. "But what we learned is that we don't live forever. That, at some point, everything dies. And the way Mr. Leach explained it, one day, you'll be an empty package. But it won't be you. Oh, I can't explain it either," he said, exasperated. "Let's just say that at some point, you won't be living anymore. So, we have some questions: If we are not here forever, then where do we go when we die? Mr. Leach says this is a mystery. But if we're here for only a certain amount of time, I keep thinking we should be *doing* something . . . I don't know . . . something special, something important, something so that when we do die and are not here any longer, it won't be like we were never here."

"Yeah," Niles added. "What have I done with my life? I eat and sleep, eat and sleep. What kind of a life is that?"

"A dog's life!" Poppy laughed.

"C'mon Poppy. Don't you understand?" Niles pleaded.

Poppy puffed up, then kind of shimmied all over and flapped her wings, creating a commotion entirely unexpected and sending puffs of down into the air that floated about her, like snow slowly falling to the ground. Niles and Nathaniel stepped back again, somewhat alarmed.

"I'm thinking," Poppy explained.

"Oh, you do that when you think?" Niles asked.

"Do what?" she asked, not really paying attention.

"Never mind," Nathaniel said and hushed Niles.

Poppy remained silent for a while, which Niles and Nathaniel interpreted as more thinking when suddenly, she started pecking again at Niles's dog tag.

"Hey, watch it, Poppy!" Niles said and jumped back.

"Oh, sorry. It's so shiny and pretty. Lost in my thoughts. Love that. Where did you get that?" Then, before he could answer, she puffed up again, shook, and flapped her wings twice more and said, "I will join you. Or . . . I guess I should ask if I may join you. I think you have asked a good question! If our lives are only for a short time, then how we spend this time should mean *something.*"

"Hey, that's it! You said it just right," Nathaniel said. "So the question is, if we are here for only a short while, how should we then live? I like it. And sure, you can join us! But we can't fly, so are you going to walk with us," he added, a little puzzled.

"And you can't walk the wires, Niles, but you still are able to journey together, right?" Poppy reasoned.

"Yeah, of course," Niles answered.

"I'm not going to walk," she said. "That's silly. I can help chart our direction. I can scout ahead so we are prepared for any dangers. Where are we headed, anyway?"

Niles and Nathaniel looked at one another and then back at Poppy and shrugged.

Poppy squawked out a hearty laugh, and Nathaniel and Niles joined in.

"Who knows?" laughed Nathaniel. "But right now, I'm hungry. Let's eat."

They stopped near the same house where Nathaniel had foraged through the garbage can the night before and found still more uneaten leftovers, which Nathaniel shared with Niles. Poppy was content to sit in a nearby tree where she picked over its fruit, all the while mumbling and squawking to herself.

After they all finished eating, Poppy flew to a branch in a shrub next to Niles and Nathaniel. "So, now what?" she asked.

Niles looked back and forth between Nathaniel and Poppy. "Poppy," he said, "I've been thinking. We're not sure where we should go or who we should talk to next. I mean, who can explain to us how to live the life we were meant to live? I mean, who can tell anyone how to live his life?"

"But you're not really looking to have someone tell you how to live your life," said Poppy. "It's more like . . . well, the world is so big and complicated. And, now that I think about it, we are here for maybe a short time and then, one day . . . poof, we're gone. What's the point of that!?" Poppy extended her wings and shrugged. "I think we're supposed to do *something* while we are here, right? Otherwise, nothing matters. You're born, then you die."

"Yeah, and nobody remembers anybody," Nathaniel added. "Like, eh, who was that Yorkie? I think his name was Niles." He scratched his chin thoughtfully, then looked over at Niles with a smile.

"Be quiet, Nathaniel. I'll be remembered." Niles moved closer to Nathaniel, wagging his head as he spoke. "I'll be remembered for the way I lived my life!"

"Oh yeah?" Nathaniel teased.

"Yeah, really! C'mon you guys!" Niles pleaded. "It should matter what you do between your when you start and when you finish, shouldn't it? I mean that's your life, right? What have you done with it? But the problem we have right now is knowing *what* to do with that space in between." Then, turning to Poppy, Niles abruptly said, "What about you, Poppy? You're the one with the best view on things. You're so sophisticated. You're the worldly one, so tell us where to go and who to talk to in order to live the life we were meant to live."

"Yeah, Poppy. You have the *big* picture from way up there." Nathaniel gestured expansively toward the sky. "I bet you could show us a thing or two about how to really live. What about it, Poppy? Where do we go next?"

Poppy remained quiet for a few moments, seeming to contemplate Nathaniel's question. Both Nathaniel and Niles watched as she unconsciously puffed herself up into a green and red and yellow feathered ball once again. Then she violently shook herself several times and wildly flapped her wings, again causing a great commotion that drove Niles and Nathaniel to the ground this time. Then, all was quiet as little clouds of down floated in the air surrounding the three of them, slowly falling one by one to the ground below.

Poppy flew from the branch, landed in front of Niles and Nathaniel, cocked her head first to one side, then the other, and finally pecked a few times at Niles's dog tag. Niles was no longer alarmed by this behavior and said, "I know, Poppy. Shiny objects, right?"

"I have an idea," Poppy said thoughtfully. "There is a place I have seen that is unlike any place I have ever seen before. It is an entirely different world inhabited by unusual creatures with magical powers. It is a world of water. A body of water that is so great that it is impossible to know where it ends or even *if* it ends. Many say it does go on forever. They call it *the sea,* and it's filled with many extraordinary creatures who live there."

"Live there?" said Nathaniel. "By 'live there,' you mean they live *in* water?" He looked puzzled.

"That's right," Poppy answered. "Their world is *under* the water, which is why I told you these are magical creatures. Somewhere they have learned the magic of breathing under water."

"That's impossible!" Niles said, incredulous. Then he whined, "Oh no, this is making my head hurt again."

"I think it is reasonable to conclude that any creature capable of such magic must know a great deal about many things, including how to live your life well." Poppy spoke these words quietly, as if she were engaged in some sort of internal dialogue, but then directed her attention to Niles and Nathaniel. "What do you think?" she asked.

"I don't know." Niles said cautiously. "It sounds very odd to me. How do you know these creatures if you say they live in an underwater world, Poppy?"

"I don't know these sea creatures. I know *of* them," Poppy answered.

"Okay," Nathaniel said hesitantly.

"Okay?" Poppy looked Niles and Nathaniel up and down. "Okay? Is that all you have to say? Okay? Are you serious about all this…about this *quest,* as you called it?"

"Sure we are, Poppy!" said Niles. "Right, Nathaniel?"

"Yep, yep. We are. We sure are!" Nathaniel was shaken by the intensity of Poppy's response to their hesitation and didn't want to be seen as not up to the task.

Poppy continued speaking. "I have seen the sea only once and kept my distance because it frightened me. It is so big, and the idea that there are creatures in it that I couldn't see because they were under the water seemed too strange for me to bear."

Niles and Nathaniel nodded in agreement.

"But if I had help." Poppy's voice trailed off and she seemed to ponder this for a moment. Then as if her thoughts had organized themselves she spoke decisively. "There is a community of birds known as the gulls that I have seen before but have never met. They live near the sea and, I believe, even communicate with the sea's creatures. I'm told they know the sea very well and have no fear of it. If we can get to the sea, maybe my brother and sister gulls will help us."

Nathaniel leaped to his feet and proclaimed, "Then onward! To the sea!"

Poppy smiled and leaned close to Nathaniel. "Found your courage?" she asked.

Nathaniel gritted his teeth, ready to scold Poppy for what he thought was an uncalled for remark, but he thought better of it when she turned back to him, winked, and smiled.

# CHAPTER 5

• • •

# To The Sea!

POPPY FLEW AHEAD, circling back from time to time to be sure Niles and Nathaniel were following her lead. Daytime travel presented a number of awkward challenges. First, Nathaniel *was*, after all, a rat, and humans, as a rule, do not like or are repelled by rats. Second, Niles would likely be seen as a lost dog, and some well-intended human might think he was doing Niles a favor by capturing him and hauling him away to the animal control center. The stories that circulated about animal control were hair-raising, and Niles had no intention of learning whether or not these stories were true.

Third, Niles and Nathaniel were unlikely buddies, and a dog and a rat conspicuously traveling together would bring unnecessary attention. So, Nathaniel did his best to remain inconspicuous by walking the wires where possible or seeking the cover of the shrubs that lined the walkways in some of the residential areas through which they passed. Niles did his best to take directional cues from Poppy and Nathaniel but periodically became confused about exactly where his friends were and sometimes felt quite lost. More than a few times, he won the sympathy of those who saw him looking perplexed.

"Oh, look at that cute Yorkie," a passerby would say. "I bet she's lost." And then they would try to coax him in squeaky, high voices to come closer. "Hi there, cutie. C'mon girl. Here girl!" They'd snap their fingers and clap their hands. Niles found it best to feign indifference and pass quickly through the area as if he had permission to be off his leash.

Around midday, they saw that they would have to walk through a section of town where a number of restaurants had sidewalk tables with people enjoying their meals outdoors. Niles padded by them, conveying the confidence of a dog who was accustomed to being on his own and alone in such a busy part of town. Nathaniel, who had darted from shrub to shrub up to this point, had no way to follow Niles without exposing himself. There were no overhead wires and no way to hide himself if he was going to stay close to Niles.

Niles moved confidently along the sidewalk, enjoying the smells of cooked meat while forgetting to check that Nathaniel was following him. The gap between them widened more and more as Nathaniel hesitated under a shrub. Knowing full well that making a run for it might create pandemonium, Nathaniel sized up just how far he would have to run entirely exposed to those enjoying their lunch.

Niles had now disappeared from Nathaniel's sight so, he thought, it was now or never. He took a few deep breathes and bolted across the distance and under the tables of those who had been enjoying their lunches. He ran as fast as his legs could carry him but was spotted immediately while scrambling under the outdoor tables, setting off an hysterical chain reaction of shrieks, screams, and outrage.

"Oh my God, it's a rat!"

Some people jumped up from their seats, and others tried kicking him.

"I can't believe it," they shouted.

"How disgusting!"

"I'm never eating here again!"

Hearing the shrieks and commotion, Niles turned around just in time to see Nathaniel hustling to escape the chaos he had created, running his way as fast as he could.

"Hurry! Hurry!" Niles barked.

When Nathaniel caught up with Niles, they ducked under a shrub where Nathaniel gulped for air while Niles laughed and laughed.

"Happens every time!" Nathaniel said between breaths. "What is it with humans and rats? I'm not such a bad-looking guy, right?" he asked plaintively.

"You're a fine looking rat, Nathaniel," Niles said most sincerely.

"I just don't get the respect I deserve." Nathaniel chuckled.

Poppy had flown on ahead to determine whether they would make it to the sea by nightfall. As the wind currents changed, she knew she was very close. Finally, she spotted it, blue-green and extending infinitely beyond the horizon. While she knew *of* the gulls, she had never encountered them because she preferred to remain inland with the members of her own community, where food was plentiful. There was little reason for her to be near the sea, and that was not lost on the three gulls who sailed high above her and discerned that she was unaccustomed to riding the winds. Poppy was awestruck by the elegance of their streamlined shape, their long wings, and how effortlessly they remained aloft. The gulls rose and fell on the wind currents as if they were riding invisible waves. By comparison, she was embarrassed that her flying skills looked clumsy and labored as she struggled to manage the sea breezes.

"Hellooo, hellooo."

The haunting call of the gulls seemed to sail upon and become one with the wind.

"Hellooo, loo, loo. Hellooo, loo, loo," they called. Their tones carried a note of sadness, Poppy thought.

Finally, exhausted by the effort of remaining airborne in the face of strong headwinds, Poppy shouted into the wind, "Please, I hope you can help me. But I am tired and must find a place to rest."

The gulls nodded their understanding and said, "Followww, followww!"

They sailed toward the beach, landing on the sand set back away from the crashing waves. Poppy landed inelegantly in front of them, where she paused to capture her breath. As her breathing slowed, she smiled, thinking that the gulls looked rather silly standing there on the sand, all feet and beak and sort of, well, goofy.

The three gulls cocked their heads, waiting for Poppy to speak. Just as she was about to explain her request, several more gulls arrived, and then three more and four more and five more. One of them called out, "What's going on? Is it something to eat?"

There was a great deal of confusion about who had found what to eat as still more of the gulls arrived. Finally, one of the original three gulls that Poppy had spoken to asked for silence. The number of gulls had grown considerably, and Poppy, standing in the middle of what was now a crowd, was a bit uneasy as she began to speak.

"I have come to ask your assistance on behalf of my friends," she began. The crowd of gulls encircled Poppy and listened attentively. "My two friends and I are on a quest to understand what seems to be a great mystery."

There were nods and sounds of approval from the crowd. "Yes, yes. Please go on," they encouraged.

"My fellow sojourners tell me that they have discovered that life is not without end but, indeed, rather short."

There were whispers among the crowd, some expressions of wonder, and others of disbelief.

One of the gulls, who, oddly enough, was missing both an eye and a foot, nodded his head in agreement, saying, "I have heard this is true. Please continue, young lady."

Poppy turned away from the wounded gull, not wishing to stare or be rude. "My friends and I believe that if life is short and uncertain, then we should live our lives a certain way; in a meaningful way. As my friends say, we want to *really* live, although I must confess I'm uncertain what that means."

"Why have you come to us?" the one-legged gull asked.

"I have come to you because wisdom grows from one's ability to see the world more completely. My friend Niles has lived his entire life in a small home with a small yard."

Some of the gulls laughed. "What could he possibly know? He hasn't seen the world. Certainly, he could not know what we know."

"That's right. I agree. My other friend Nathaniel walks the wires behind the homes up on the hill," she said, indicating inland. "His perspective is far greater than Niles's but still less than my own. And from my perspective, I see still more than either of my friends but cannot tell them what it means to really live."

"Why, this is a silly quest," one of the young gulls spoke up.

A few others nodded their agreement, and still others scoffed at her words.

"It's nonsense," said another.

Soon, the gulls were arguing among themselves and there was a good deal of wing flapping and name calling until finally, the crowd began to disperse in a fit of noisy squabbling. In a very short time, Poppy found herself alone except for the half blind, one-legged gull who laughed as she looked around.

"Where have they all gone?" the old gull asked.

Poppy looked at the old gull and shook her head. "Maybe this is silly," she said.

"What do you want?" the gull asked.

She looked at the old gull and said as earnestly as she could, "Perhaps to summon a creature from the sea to ask them if they might tell us how to really live."

"Why?" he asked.

"Because the sea is so vast! It is infinite, and I am told there are creatures who live under the sea who must be very wise to have unlocked the mystery of how to live underwater." She laughed and added, "Any creature capable of this sort of miracle must understand things better than we do!"

"Hmm. Good point," the gull conceded. "I do know some of these creatures, and, well, I don't know. But I will try to help. You may be correct. What is your name?"

"I am Poppy," she answered. Then she started to say something and stopped.

"Go on," the gull encouraged, "you want to ask me what happened?"

"How did you know I was. . . ?" Poppy started to ask.

"Don't worry. I know. I lost both my eye and foot when I carelessly tried to steal bait from a fishing boat. I became entangled in the fishing line of a young fisherman—actually a boy—when he cast it toward the water. The hook caught me right in the eye. They reeled me in like a crazed fish and removed the hook, but the line had wrapped itself tight around my leg. I carried that fishing line wrapped around my leg wherever I went for the longest time. I lost feeling in the leg and became very sick. That's when *I* learned that life doesn't go on forever. I was so sick, I'm sure I was delirious. Late one evening, I was laying in some tall grass for protection and struggling with the pain when I was visited by a possum, of all things, who spoke to me about death. It was the strangest thing. I can't remember what he called himself, but I do remember that he kept grinning and grinning. I thought, *What's to be happy about?* Anyway, it may have been a dream, but it sure changed my thinking."

Poppy was astonished by this coincidence, puffed herself up and quaked all over. Then, wildly flapping her wings several times, she said, "Yes," and nothing more.

The gull turned to carefully examine Poppy with his good eye. "Yes?" he asked.

"Yes," Poppy answered, feeling as if she was now understood.

The gull looked at Poppy kindly. She eyed him up and down. A missing eye, only one leg, and generally rather haggard but patient and gentle, and, most importantly, he was kind to her.

"I am Bela, Poppy," said the gull. "Now, you should go find your friends and bring them to the foot of the jetty out there." He pointed his beak toward a chain of large rocks that extended hundreds of feet out to the sea. "We will meet this evening, just after the sun sets and most of my community is nesting."

Poppy was both tired and hungry, but it was late afternoon, and she had to find Niles and Nathaniel so they could meet Bela at the jetty after sundown. She flew back in the direction where she had seen them last and found nothing. She flew over the restaurants they would have had to pass and over the sidewalks they most likely would have taken to follow the direction she had provided them. Still, nothing. Then she passed over a park where a group of children were

playing on a jungle gym and slide. What must have been one of the children's parents was near the hedge by the sidewalk holding out what looked like half a hamburger. And immediately in front of her was a small dog that may have been Niles, though Poppy wasn't sure.

Poppy looped one time around, coming in low, when the dog's metal tag caught the glint of the afternoon sun, capturing and holding her attention. Niles, completely unaware of the incoming bird, was munching on the half of the hamburger the woman had apparently shared with him. As she swooped in low, she screeched, "I love shiny objects!".

Niles looked up just in time to yelp as the bird made a grab for his dog tag. "Niles! *It's you!*" she shouted over her wing as she ascended once again.

Niles barked and Poppy screeched at the same time at one another: "*What are you doing*?!"

"What the. . . ?!" shouted the woman with half a hamburger. Then, calling to the children climbing on the jungle gym, "Did you kids see that? A parrot! A crazy parrot just tried to attack this poor dog."

The woman tried to pick up Niles who wriggled free and called frantically for Nathaniel. Of course, all the woman saw and heard was Niles jumping about and barking.

"What parrot?" asked the children. "What parrot? Where's the parrot, mom?"

The children, now running to their mother, were delighted. But it was too late, and Nathaniel, who had been napping under the shrub, heard Niles's call and was now scrambling after Poppy, who flew very close to the walk that led them away from the park and into a residential area.

Once safe, they settled into the rhythm one finds when they are hiking and talked about nothing especially important.

"I'm hungry," Nathaniel complained.

"I'm tired," Niles answered.

"Well, at least you got some of that lady's hamburger, and what did I get?" Nathaniel whined.

"You got some rest. So where does that leave us? You hungry and me tired, okay?"

Poppy circled back, flying low over her friends, and shouted as she passed, "Knock it off, you guys. I'm tired *and* hungry, but we meet Bela at sundown. So we eat and rest later!" Then off she went on ahead.

Niles turned to Nathaniel and asked, "Who's Bela?"

Nathaniel shrugged and said, "She sounds pretty serious, so we'd better pick up the pace."

By late afternoon, they found themselves on a street at the top of a hill with a direct shot to the sea. The canopy of leaves from the trees that lined the street obscured their vision, but Poppy assured them that the touch of blue they saw at the very end of the street was the sea and they could smell something wholly different from those they were familiar with, so they found their second wind and hurried along. They followed the road for the better part of an hour until, at last, they came to a bluff that overlooked a sandy beach with the sea beyond it.

# CHAPTER 6

• • •

# The Gulls

POPPY LANDED NEXT to Niles, who now stood between her and Nathaniel. They stood silently, looking out at the sea. The breeze off the sea was fresh and salty. Niles and Nathaniel's noses could be seen to twitch as each registered this delightfully new and exotic fragrance. Niles's hair, which normally hung in front of his eyes, was blown back by the sea breezes, forcing him to squint as the sun sat low on the sea's horizon. Waves crashed below in a hypnotic sort of rhythm that both of them found soothing.

"I've never seen anything so beautiful!" Niles whispered as he took it all in. "It goes on forever and looks as though it is about to swallow the sun," he continued. "Don't you think so?" he asked no one in particular.

In unison, Nathaniel and Poppy, staring at the setting sun, answered, "Mmm."

Poppy showed them where the path to the beach was, and when they met on the sand, Niles rolled over on his back, wriggling like a worm on the sand and moaning, "Oh, this is good. Oh, this feels so good."

Nathaniel ran to the tide line where the waves reached the beach so that he could wet his feet and chimed in with his own exclamations of ecstasy. "Oh, my feet. My aching feet. The cool water is great for these poor, tired feet."

After each finished tending to their aches and pains, they gathered in a shallow, hollowed-out area under the bluff where they could not be easily seen. There, Poppy explained about Bela, the old gull with one leg and one eye. She told them he was kind, but Nathaniel was skeptical about large birds as a rule. Still, they listened carefully.

"What will we do after we meet Bela at the foot of the jetty?" Niles asked.

"I don't know," she answered.

"Oh. . . ." Niles said somewhat tentatively.

"Remember," Nathaniel spoke up. "We can't fly! And as far as swimming is concerned? Let's just say I'd rather not." Then, looking at Niles questioningly, he said, "Well?"

"Oh," Niles answered, looking concerned. "I don't think I can swim very well."

"And I don't think you need to worry." Poppy seemed very much in charge, and this gave both Niles and Nathaniel a greater feeling of confidence. "This gull is trustworthy, I believe. Now, we have time to rest and eat before dark. Nathaniel, I spotted a trash can back towards the path to the bluff. Why don't you go see what you can find to eat? I also saw some fruit trees just over the bluff. I'm starved." Then, she indicated the small, hollowed-out area that was perhaps a bit too small to call a cave but provided decent cover and added, "Niles, why don't you rest here? No one will see you, and the beach seems quiet enough."

Nathaniel and Poppy set out, leaving Niles alone under the bluff. Niles was restless and worried about many things and so found it difficult to get comfortable. He had no real sense of time or how long he had been gone from MAN and Mama, but he missed them, as well as Geddes and Tamar. He played and replayed the encounter with the owl in his head, shuddering to think what might have happened to Nathaniel. He worried that this journey . . . this—what had he called it? This *quest* was itself without any purpose. But even as he wondered about these things, he felt a restlessness deep down that he was squandering his life. What he wrestled with was the desire to do something more with his life. He simply had no idea what that was. Finally, he lay down and fell into an uneasy sleep where his worries seemed to follow.

Again, as before, the silver cat with the icy blue eyes beckoned. She called his name several times, but again, as previously, her mouth never moved, so he wondered if it was Deheune or his imagination. She sat at the entrance to the hollowed-out area under the bluff where Niles slept. Her tail, as before, moved in and around her feet like a snake, and she stared at Niles, slowly closing and opening those magnificent eyes, which almost illuminated the space between him and her.

"Do not be afraid, nor anxious about what has been or what is yet to come," she purred soothingly, even though she did not seem to speak. "These will only obscure your capacity to *see,* to *understand,* and to *know* what *you must do now.*"

> *"Be still now, indifferent to what was or is to be;*
> *Release what you wish were true or simply hope to see.*
> *The moment now your guide, informing you what's right;*
> *Your teacher, your master, your beacon, your light.*
> *Yet examine the moment from every which way,*
> *To know what to do, to inform what you say."*

Niles wanted desperately to ask questions, to seek clarification, but found himself unable to speak. So he sat, silently looking into her jewel-blue eyes, and a vague sensation of understanding washed over him. But the sensation

was pure feeling and escaped explanation, so he sat wordlessly. As strange as all this was, it felt so real to Niles that he wondered whether he was dreaming or not. Then she purred again, and in her eyes, Niles felt he detected the hint of a smile.

# CHAPTER 7

• • •

# The Dolphins

NILES WAS AWAKENED by the sound of Nathaniel munching on a browning apple core.

"You hungry?" he asked and gestured to an oil-stained, brown paper sack that sat at the entrance to where they had taken shelter. There was a collection of broken potato chips in the bag along with the crusts from a sandwich in a clear plastic baggie. Niles, still disoriented from the dream, considered saying something to Nathaniel about his dream but didn't know how to put it into words. This was the third time he'd dreamed about this cat, and even though the dreams themselves were pleasant, they were confusing.

"What's up?" Nathaniel asked with a mouth full of apple. "Something on your mind?"

Niles looked at Nathaniel quizzically, his head turned to one side.

Nathaniel stopped chewing. "Well? What?"

"Nah, it's nothing." Instead of brooding, he stuck his nose in the bag and lifted his head, causing the broken potato chips to fall from the bag onto his head and into the sand. He didn't care and quickly ate them and moved on to what was left of the sandwich.

Meanwhile, Poppy had returned, and the sun was setting. Poppy was pre-occupied and chattering to herself about something that neither Niles nor Nathaniel could make out. Finally, she said that they should make their way to the jetty, which was several hundred yards down the beach. She would fly on ahead and meet Bela at the foot of the jetty.

"You boys need to get a move on, and I'll wait for you there," she said.

Poppy flew off in the direction of the jetty while Niles and Nathaniel began hiking their way across the sand. Neither had ever walked on sand before, and the going was slow as the sand gave way under their feet with each step, making what they thought would be a short hike a particularly exhausting one.

The jetty was a huge collection of rocks of varying size piled one on the other, creating a pier of sorts that extended like a finger about 150 yards from the sandy beach out into the sea. They arrived, panting and exhausted, to find Poppy standing on one of the rocks at the top of the jetty above the sand.

"Here comes Bela," Poppy shouted down to them. It was difficult to hear over the waves breaking on both sides of the jetty as well as a fairly strong wind that blew off the sea.

"Hard to hear what you said," Niles yelled back up to Poppy when Bela dropped into their line of sight, calling, "Helooo, loo. Heloooo, loo."

Bela hung suspended in the air before them, his long wings outstretched, effortlessly riding the wind off the sea. "Helooo, loo," he called again to them as he landed on a rock alongside Poppy. Niles and Nathaniel saw that they would have to climb the rocks to get to the top of the jetty, which was no easy task since the gaps between the rocks often required daring leaps that were especially challenging for Nathaniel.

At the top of the jetty, Poppy introduced Niles and Nathaniel to Bela.

"Why do you only have one leg?" Niles asked.

"Niles!" Poppy scolded, clearly annoyed with Niles's impolite question.

"No, no, it's fine," Bela responded patiently. Then, turning to Niles, he laughed and said, "I'm missing an eye too!"

Startled by this, Niles swallowed hard and stood straight and was unable to avert his eyes even as he wanted to.

"Oh, listen dear, I have been around too long to be bothered by something as small as a couple of curious creatures," said Bela. "These boys have just seen seagulls for the first time ever, so a one-eyed, one-legged seagull must be something of a curiosity, eh? Well, I'm something of a novelty among the gulls. Most of them have a pair of eyes and legs, but I do get along just fine." He paused for a moment as if remembering something, then turned to face Poppy with his good eye. "You never asked why I remained when all the other gulls left after hearing your request for help."

"Well, I was, you know, just happy you listened," Poppy said, a little embarrassed. She felt as if he had read her mind because she *did* wonder why he had stayed.

"Well, it's all a part of the same story I guess," he continued. "As to *what* happened; it was just as I told Poppy. I *say* it was a fishing accident." He laughed quietly and went on. "My leg was tangled in fishing line, and the eye was put out when a fishhook caught me right there. It was quite a mess. Perhaps I should have known better than to be looking for a handout from one of the fishing boats. But it was a boy who wildly cast his line while I hovered behind their boat. Caught me in the eye, and it hurt like the devil! In all my thrashing about, my leg was entangled in the line. When they brought me aboard, they cut out the hook but left the line around my leg. As I say, it was a messy business."

He turned his head so Niles and Nathaniel saw clearly now that he had a blackened hole where his eye had been. Their curiosity was greater than their manners, and they stared for a moment, imagining the horror of such an accident and shuddering at the thought.

"Don't be rude!" Poppy whispered quite sternly.

"No, it's okay. Take a look, boys," Bela responded casually. "I don't mind if others look or ask questions because these wounds have made me a better gull . . . a better creature."

They looked at him quizzically.

"Look, I'm not the first creature who has been wounded. In fact, as I got better, I started seeing things a little differently. It's ironic that I lost an eye because after this loss, I began to *see* things more clearly. More and more, I noticed as I looked around that so many have suffered wounds of one sort or another. A missing eye, a leg, a toe, an ear, a mangy dog, abandoned kittens, a broken wing. It goes on and on. The more I looked at others, the more I began to think, maybe we all have our wounds, you know? I mean, not all wounds as are as obvious as mine, right? I think sometimes the ones you can't see are the ones that maybe hurt the most.

"But here's the thing—if you're wounded, you're seen as weak. So the wounded learn to hide it. But, hidden or not, we all understand what it means to hurt. And you know what? That's the one thing we all share; gulls rats, dogs, parrots. Doesn't matter. We all have at one time or another known sadness, sorrow, and suffering. In a way, it binds us more closely together than most anything else. All created beings are united to one another because we belong to the community of the wounded."

Bela saw that the three of them regarded him skeptically and continued.

"Now don't get me wrong. . . ." Bela cocked his head and looked intensely at the three of them. "I'm not stupid. You won't hear many others agreeing with me. And here's another thing: Once you come to the realization that all of us have our burdens to bear—you know, our shortcomings, our inadequacies—why make it worse by being unkind? The unkind are those who simply never took the time to look carefully at themselves. That's what I think, and that's how I try to live my life. Hey, look, life is short and uncertain and not always easy."

At these words Niles anticipated Bela was about to explain to them how they should live, knowing that life is short and uncertain. But then he thought maybe he just had. But he struggled with trying to make sense of any life view that seemed to make a virtue of shortcomings, wounds, and weaknesses. He leaned in and waited to hear more.

"Sooner or later," Bela continued, "you're wounded by life, and it can make you angry and bitter or compassionate and kind. It's a choice, and I chose the latter. And that's why I stayed to help Poppy when the other gulls left."

The three of them looked at one another awkwardly, not knowing what to say and not even sure they understood what Bela meant. Niles avoided looking directly at Bela, looking instead at his friends and down at the rocks upon which they stood.

"Well, gosh, Bela," he said. "Thanks."

"Yeah. Well, that's that," Bela said, standing up straight on his one leg. "Tonight, we meet the dolphins, who I believe you will find know a great deal about life and may provide you with a different view on things. Their home is the sea, which, if you are at all observant, goes on forever and ever. They are extraordinary creatures, wise and happy and playful with command of these infinite waters, which are filled with extraordinary creatures." Bela laughed and continued, "Some think they are playful and happy because they are naïve, but that isn't so. I see it as a mark of their wisdom. In fact, if one creature lives playful and happy and another miserable and dour, you tell me who the wise one is."

The three of them were startled by the simplicity of Bela's ideas.

"We will need to go out further on the jetty," said Bela, "where the waters are deep and the dolphins can swim."

Undersea creatures made no sense to Niles and Nathaniel. They understood, like any other creature, what water was, but talk of anyone or anything *living* in the water seemed preposterous. That, coupled with the prospect of hiking to the end of the jetty in the middle of what was quickly becoming a cold evening, made them both weary.

The late hour and Bela's words left Niles feeling more confused than resolved. He had hoped to discover some great truth about how to live when Bela seemed to know that life did not go on forever, but his words seemed just that . . . words.

"C'mon buddy, I bet the dolphins will have some answers for us," Nathaniel whispered to Niles as they began slowly making their way further out the jetty.

"Okay," Niles answered with noticeably little enthusiasm.

Some of the jetty's rocks were great boulders while others were smaller. The uneven edges and haphazard way the rocks were piled on top of one another meant there were crevices, often quite deep, that were difficult to see in the darkness. For Poppy, it was as simple as flapping her wings, and she would cover in moments what took Nathaniel and Niles a long time. As they moved along, the water, now on both sides of the jetty and black as the night, crashed noisily against the rocks, making communication between them difficult. The waves at the end of the jetty seemed especially violent, breaking over the rocks. As each wave hit the rocks, the foamy water rushed up and around the rocks along the base of the jetty, often splashing them with the cold, salty water.

The further they went, the more harrowing it became, with strong winds that blew still more salt water in their faces while thunderous waves, one after the other, crashed at the tip of the jetty, throwing up great plumes of water and foam. As they neared the end, Bela, who seemed unmoved by the fierceness of the sea, spread his long wings and was lifted by the wind where, as if by magic, he hung suspended before them.

"Hellooo, loo," he called to them, competing with the wind, which seemed to carry his cry out to sea. "We will wait here for the dolphins."

Poppy was unused to the salt water wind and silently huddled close to Niles and Nathaniel for warmth. Niles despised the wet and cold conditions and thought how nice it would be to be cuddled on the bed between MAN and Mama, although he didn't dare speak of this to the others. Nathaniel was used to sometimes treacherous conditions, and the crevices between the dank rocks would easily meet his needs for a place to bed down while they waited, which is precisely what he did.

Poppy, who looked very uncomfortable, asked Niles if he thought the dolphins would arrive soon.

"I hope so," Niles said, gritting his teeth. And then he asked, "Poppy, are you okay?"

She smiled. "Yes, Niles, I'm okay," she answered as she tucked her beak atop her right wing and nuzzled closer to him.

While Bela skimmed the dark waters looking for the dolphins, Nathaniel and Poppy dozed, and Niles shivered in the cold. He had twice this evening suffered from coughing fits, briefly startling Poppy, whose eyes quickly again grew heavy with sleep. Niles continued to fret over many things. He now wondered if they had made a terrible mistake by trusting Bela. The ferocity of the sea frightened him, and he worried for the safety of he and his friends. He fought off his need to sleep by filling his mind with an endless parade of worries. This, together with his coughing spells, made this the most miserable night of his life, he thought. Finally, however, his continued enumeration of all his concerns against the white noise of the pounding surf lulled him to sleep.

Once again, Niles dreamed he saw the silver point Siamese with the cobalt blue eyes appear at the end of the jetty as if she had emerged from the sea. She walked toward him, climbing over the wet rocks as she approached, suggesting that it was no dream but indeed a real cat. She finally sat before Niles, close enough for him to touch her if he dared. Then she spoke in the same soothing purr and it seemed as if the thrashing sea, the salt water spray, and the cold wind all became still and faded into a backdrop for her melodic words which, again it seemed, she did not speak; he heard them not as sound but as feeling.

*"Niles. Listen,"* she said.

> *"The darkest of nights upon which you fret*
> *Not a matter of time, but your sense of regret,*
> *Shaping your thoughts, the decisions you make,*
> *Your past and your future, from which you may take*
> *Only what's gone and what is to be.*
> *Look carefully now, what do you see.*
> *Your sojourn has offered you truth all around,*
> *Yet deaf you remain, ne'er hearing the sound*
> *Of answers you seek to the question of 'how,'*
> *Of how you shall live. Live your life now."*

As in the past, there was the hint of a smile and the slow closing and opening of her blue eyes.

"Oh ho! Ha ha ha," Bela bellowed. Then, "Hellooo, loo Wake up!"

When they awoke, the sun was warm, they were dry, and there was a great deal of commotion off the side of the jetty. Nathaniel climbed from the crevice in which he slept, and Poppy flew to the side of the jetty where there was a great deal of splashing and chatter. Niles awkwardly climbed over the rocks, his whole body hurting from the past evening's coughing fits. He joined Poppy and Nathaniel to behold the strangest thing he had ever seen.

Scores of what he assumed were the "dolphins" were leaping into the air from the sea in a dance of sorts. These dolphin creatures looked like big, silver hot dogs, Niles thought.

"Ah ha!" Nathaniel yelled, delighted. "Look at them!"

They were sleek and shiny and oh so fast. Then, as if launched by some undersea catapult, they flew in great arcs through the air, laughing.

"They all seem so happy," Poppy exclaimed, delighted by the display.

"I told you they would come!" Bela shouted.

"Yes, you did!" Nathaniel shouted back.

"We never doubted it!" Niles lied.

The dolphin's acrobatics continued, much to everyone's pleasure, until a small group swam close to the jetty where they collected in a semicircle behind one of the dolphins whom Niles guessed was their leader. They sat in the water, all smiles, looking up at Niles, Nathaniel, and Poppy.

Overhead, Bela hovered and said to the dolphins, "My friends, I present to you Poppy, Nathaniel, and Niles."

As their names were called, both Niles and Nathaniel stepped forward, then back. Poppy fluttered her wings and briefly lifted herself into the air and down again.

Bela continued, "These three are on a journey . . . a quest, if you will, to discover how one should live, given their discovery that one does not live forever."

Hearing this, the dolphins all broke out in laughter, wiping the smiles from the faces of the three sojourners.

The dolphin nearest the jetty, around whom the others were gathered, spoke. "They are not laughing *at* you. Let's say they are laughing *with* you."

"I see," said Niles.

"I am Shui qi," the lead dolphin said.

"Very nice to meet you," said Niles, "but why did you laugh when Bela explained that we wanted to know how to live if life does not go on forever?"

Again, the dolphins all broke out in laughter.

Bela felt a bit embarrassed for his friends and somewhat impatiently said, "Shui qi, please tell my friends why you laugh."

Shui qi smiled for a moment and then, to everyone's astonishment, squirted Niles with a stream of water.

"Hey! Stop! Why did you do that?" Nathaniel stood on his back two legs and shook his paw at Shui qi.

Shui qi squirted some water at Nathaniel and another stream at Poppy, who were both incredulous. Shui qi just continued to smile.

"You want to know how to live?" Shui qi asked.

"Yes," Niles said and stepped forward.

"Then come closer," Shui qi directed.

Niles began climbing down the rocks close to the water's edge.

"Be careful," Poppy called after Niles.

Niles screwed up his courage and came within inches of the water, close enough to see and hear the blowhole on top of Shui qi's head. Intrigued by the way it opened and closed, he leaned a little closer when his footing slipped and he tumbled into the water.

Nathaniel, Bela, and Poppy gasped, knowing they would be unable to get him out of the water. But Niles kept his composure and dog-paddled around, and the dolphins all cheered, several of them doing great leaps in the air. Niles quickly grew tired and swallowed a little salt water that caused him to cough while he struggled to stay afloat. Shui qi dropped out of sight under the water, then rose again with Niles on his back and carried him close enough to the jetty so he could easily step back onto the rocks. Niles coughed some more, finally ending it with that terrible choking sound.

"Ack, ack, *agghhk*! There. I think I'm finished," Niles said, feeling self-conscious.

He looked much smaller and perhaps a bit pathetic while soaking wet. He heard Poppy's sympathetic cry, "Aw, poor Niles."

He looked up at her, shook himself off, and said, "I'm fine."

Again, there were cheers from the dolphins who continued smiling.

Then, looking quizzically at Shui qi, he said, "It is a puzzle to me how any creature can live *in* the water."

The dolphins laughed. Niles laughed along with them and Nathaniel, Poppy, and Bela followed his lead.

"Now I have a question for you," Shui qi answered. "How can any creature live *out* of the water?"

"Well . . . easily! Look at me. But living in and under the water. That is, well . . . miraculous." Niles smiled.

Smiling back, Shui qi said, "I see! You believe that life in the sea is a miracle while life on dry land is not?"

"Huh?" Niles looked puzzled.

"It seems you only became aware of the miracle of living in *your* world when you stumbled into *mine*? Perhaps you take for granted the air you breathe and the legs that give you mobility. You didn't seem even aware of them until you fell into the water. Is it not true that it is much easier to see the miracle of another's life while being utterly blind to the miracle of our own life?"

Niles looked back at his friends who like the others were waiting for his response. "I suppose," Niles answered hesitantly.

"Niles, to know how to live your life well, you mustn't turn away from your world to find the truth in someone else's."

"That's it?", Niles asked.

The dolphins laughed and slapped their flippers against the water as if applauding.

Niles laughed along with everyone else but found Shui qi's words perplexing, and his eyes and attention wandered, finally fixing on the hole atop Shui qi's head.

"So you live in water but breathe air?" said Niles. "And so that's why you have that um . . . er—that hole on the top of your head?" Niles asked awkwardly.

"Indeed!" Shui qi answered and then blew a sound like that of a trumpet, evoking still more laughter. "You fail to appreciate the miracle of your own life while seeing the miracle of ours. The sea is filled with creatures who take no notice of the water in which they dwell any more than you have taken notice of the world in which *you* dwell. They fail to see what surrounds them because they are asleep. How can one live well while they remain asleep? Perhaps the answer to your question is right in front of you, but you are *asleep*!" Again, Shui qi laughed a hearty laugh, and the other dolphins joined in.

Niles joined the dolphins, thinking it was all absurdly funny. Soon, Nathaniel, Poppy, and Bela were laughing along too.

Shui qi and the other dolphins held their heads above water, laughing as they backed away from the jetty. There, they were joined by the others, and again there were grand displays of acrobatic feats to delight their audience until Shui qi swam close to the jetty again.

"You must *wake up*, my friend. Because if you cannot see the miracle of your own existence, you are clearly asleep," he said rather sternly. "Listen to my words friends, 'Wake up!' Look at all you have but as yet have not seen! It is a miracle, but you will see it only if you wake up."

As he said this, he swam to meet the other members of their merry parade, leaping and laughing, heading toward . . . who knew?

Still laughing, Bela opened his great wings and allowed the wind to carry him aloft. He rose just a few feet over Niles, Nathaniel, and Poppy and said, "Maybe what's so complicated about this is that the answers are uncomplicated and obvious. What's the expression? 'Hiding in plain sight?' Looking for what is simple in a mountain of complexities. Time for me to go now, too. Remember to be kind and compassionate to all creatures. They're carrying a heavy burden."

"But wait!" shouted Poppy as Bela was allowing the wind to carry him up, up, up. "Where do we go now?"

Bela was gliding high above them now among the other gulls, perhaps too high up to have heard Poppy. All they heard was, *"Hellooo, loo."* But that could have been from any of the gulls soaring high above them.

Two days had passed since they'd met the dolphins. Niles continued having more frequent fits of coughing ever since falling into the sea. After Shui qi and Bela left them, they were at loose ends regarding what to do and where to go next, so they decided to return to familiar territory—Niles's and Nathaniel's neighborhood.

The climb up the hill was difficult for Niles, who was now becoming easily winded, forcing them to stop frequently in residential areas where it was difficult for the three of them to travel together. After two days of spending restless nights in people's yards and eating nothing but avocados, Niles felt terrible. Their aim, they decided, was to seek out a place where Niles could rest and recover and then decide how to proceed.

They chose a different route back to their neighborhood to avoid the string of outdoor cafes where earlier Nathaniel had upset the diners and nearly gotten trampled. Instead, they took a more remote route through grassy fields, arriving at a place that neither felt nor smelled familiar.

It was early afternoon when they came to the crest of a hill where before them were acres and acres of beautifully groomed green grass. Best of all, the area seemed abandoned, even though the noise of traffic could be readily heard from the roads below. They hiked across the grass until they spotted a small vehicle carrying several men. It was a strange thing they did next—the men got out of their vehicle pulled a stick-like instrument from a bag in the rear of the vehicle and swung the stick furiously at what Poppy thought might be an egg. Thankfully, the egg was hard enough not to break, but it went flying through the air, landing somewhere further down the field of green grass. They were aghast and, indeed, frightened by these violent stick-wielding men bent on smashing this egg.

"I say we get out of here as fast as we can," Nathaniel said, already surveying the landscape for a better place to rest. He pointed back down the other side of the hill. "Look. The grass over there is tall, and we won't be seen. It's a good-sized canyon, and there will be plenty of safer places to stay."

When Niles and Nathaniel looked for Poppy to give her consent, they realized she wasn't there. She arrived, out of breath, only seconds after their initial alarm over her absence.

"Those men!" she said. She halted a moment to catch her breath. "They chased the very same eggs they hit before and battered them yet again! I couldn't watch. They were brutal." She shook her head, baffled by the things she had seen. "We should move quickly to someplace safer!"

Niles and Nathaniel found a trail that led into the grassy canyon, and Poppy flew on ahead to see if she could find a suitable camp for them.

Poppy found a shallow, tan sandstone cave that would provide shelter and protection after they improvised with some camouflage. The only challenge this plan presented was that the canyon was on the other side of a very busy road. Crossing any street was a harrowing experience, and since learning that life didn't go on forever, they had taken notice of the failed efforts of other creatures whose remains had been embedded in the asphalt. Fortunately, later that evening, Poppy was able to give the "coast is clear" sign from above the road when there was a lull in the traffic. Still, they ran as fast as they could, and just moments after they made it to the other side, two bright lights and the roar of a passing big rig, followed by a wind that nearly knocked Nathaniel over, was a vivid reminder of the dangers of road crossings.

"Hurry! This way," Poppy urged as she indicated the entrance to a narrow trail through the tall grass.

Soon, they were impossible to see from anywhere on the ground, although, as Poppy could attest, they were quite visible from above, including to any creature standing at the top of the canyon ridge. About halfway up the canyon path, Poppy directed them off the trail and toward the canyon wall where they found the shallow cave Poppy had identified earlier.

Hungry and exhausted, Niles and Nathaniel knew that only Poppy was in a position to get something to eat, and so Nathaniel gnawed off bunches of grass to help make a bed while Niles scratched the sandy floor of the cave, creating an indentation into which he snuggled, Nathaniel on a bed of grass by his side. Poppy did not fly away to eat but instead perched in a bush outside the cave, tucked her beak into the soft place between her wings, and soon was asleep.

Sometime that night, Deheune came to Niles, not silently or gently, but with a greater sense of urgency than ever before.

"Niles," she called.

Niles wasn't sure if he woke only in his dream or actually woke up and saw Deheune, who appeared to him much larger than she had in other encounters. Her voice was not persuasive, as it had been previously, but authoritative and her directions clear.

"Niles, leave the cave where you now sleep and climb to the top of the canyon where you will find a grassy bluff. Follow the sounds to the street and cross it. It is late, and there will be little danger of moving vehicles. Once you have crossed the street, you will notice many strange and unusual scents. Follow the scents until you come to a place where you will find many creatures such as you have never known."

> *"Do not be fooled by this place of captivity,*
> *A lively palace of intellectual activity*
> *And souls whose wisdom you, my friend, lack.*
> *So, sit at the feet of the great silverback."*

When Niles woke, the sky was dark and the canyon quiet except for the gentle rustling of the grass caused by a light wind and the faint sound of traffic in the distance. Poppy, whose beak was nuzzled into her back, opened an eye and watched Niles for a moment. Without moving her beak, she asked Niles what was wrong, although her voice was muffled as if she were speaking into a pillow.

"We have to go . . . now," Niles explained, his voice tense and hoarse.

Poppy turned her head to Niles. "Why?"

"Because we have to. Please don't ask. Just trust me on this," Niles said, nudging Nathaniel, who was already awake.

"Okay, buddy," said Nathaniel. "I trust you. Where are we going?"

"Up to the top of the canyon to the grassy bluff where we'll cross the street, and I'll. . . ." Niles thought it would sound ridiculous for him to say that then they would wait for Niles to pick up the scent of . . . what? Niles didn't finish his sentence. Instead, he said, "Let's go."

Poppy quickly flew to the top of the canyon and saw the grassy bluff and the street some ways beyond that. She puzzled over how Niles could have known what was at the top of the hill.

The climb was a rigorous one, especially for Nathaniel, who, when he reached the top, was winded.

"Ok," Nathaniel huffed. "So now what?"

"The street is just a short way from here," Poppy explained. They could hear the occasional vehicle making its way up to the top of the hill where they planned to cross, but Poppy, flying well above the street, kept a sharp eye out for traffic and shouted "*Clear*!" when they could safely cross the street to the other side—the side where Deheune had told Niles he would pick up some sort of strange scent.

It was darker on this side of the street, and Niles lifted his snout in the air and began sniffing.

"What are you doing?" Nathaniel asked.

"Shh," Niles hushed him. "I'm searching for a scent."

"What sort of scent?" Poppy whispered.

Niles shook his head. "I don't know," he said impatiently.

Poppy cocked her head and looked over at Nathaniel with wide eyes; Nathaniel returned the gesture.

As they walked forward, it grew darker and darker. It was difficult to see, and Niles soon stumbled over a chain that was swaged between a line of posts in front a row of hedges.

"Wait! There it is!" he said. Niles stood still his nose poked in the air, sniffing wildly. "What is this?!" he shouted, sounding at once exhilarated and frustrated.

The scent Niles picked up was a wild spectrum of smells, none of which were familiar to him. He walked past the chain and through the hedges until he came to a wrought iron fence whose bars were just far enough apart that he could barely squeeze between them. Nathaniel followed Niles, and Poppy followed Nathaniel, although she felt silly walking when she could easily have flown over the fence.

On the other side of the fence was a walkway dimly lit with small streetlamps that traced a path leading to their right and their left.

Niles sniffed the air, which was electric with peculiar scents, and shook his head saying, "Well, let's go this way."

He headed to the right, which climbed up a hill and swung to the left. Poppy flew above them, slowly surveying what she saw below, and knew that Niles and Nathaniel could not see from their vantage point what she was seeing: She flew over enclosure after enclosure, each containing animals of all kinds, some of them asleep, some of them awake and pacing nervously. Shaken by the sight, she quickly swooped in before Niles and Nathaniel and told them what she saw.

"That explains all these unusual scents that are driving me crazy," Niles said, relieved. "But I want to see for myself."

"Me too," Nathaniel chimed in.

Soon, they came to enclosures where only glass separated them from the captive animals. They were stunned by the size and unusual characteristics of some of the animals they saw. The elephants were a complete mystery to them, with legs as big as trees and noses that seemed to be creatures unto themselves.

Nathaniel nudged Niles and pointed to the chains that bound the elephants. "Why do you think. . . ?" Niles started to ask. Then he shouted in the direction of the three elephants, "Excuse me, ah . . . sir."

One of the elephants flapped his great ears back and forth and slowly turned its mighty, gnarled, gray head in Niles's direction and squinted to see who had spoken.

"Hello, little dog." The elephant spoke in a deep, weary, but unmistakably female voice. "I see you have friends." The elephant offered a sleepy smile. "Hello, little dog's friends."

Niles thought this was one of the most unusual creatures he had ever seen. Its tail appeared to be connected to its face, and it extended in Niles's direction. He leaped back, fearing it might swallow him.

"Ah ha," he said. "Excuse me. Yes, I do have my friends with me . . . ah—er—ma'am . . . miss."

"Call me Gemma."

"Okay, Gemma. So, I am confused. I have never met anyone quite like you and your friends. Who are you? What is this place? And why are there chains around your legs?" Niles spoke hurriedly, partly because he was nervous and, again, because he had many questions and was eager for answers.

"Little dog, manners . . . please!" Gemma chided Niles. Gemma's two companions snorted. "Let's begin with your name. And did you have any plans to introduce your friends?"

"Oh, I'm sorry," said Niles. "It's just that I. . . . Well, my name is Niles, and these are my friends Poppy and Nathaniel."

One of the elephants next to Gemma said to the other, in a voice loud enough for all to hear, "Isn't that tiny one a rat, dear?"

"Actually a fruit rat!" Nathaniel called out.

"What's that he said?" one elephant asked the other.

"He says he's a fruit rat?" The two elephants chortled.

"Oh, forget it," Nathaniel threw his hands down in frustration.

"Easy, Nathaniel," Niles whispered over his shoulder. Then, returning his attention to Gemma, he said, "So, this place is. . . ? And the chains?"

"Well, this is a zoo, of course," Gemma said with some impatience. "And the chains are to keep us from wandering into the city. We are not very good on the bus or in the supermarket, you know."

"And who'd clean up after us?" called one of the two elephants who continued to stand with her back to Niles and his friends.

"Oh, I see," Niles said very seriously.

The three elephants laughed uproariously.

"Oh, little Niles, you mustn't be so gullible," said Gemma. "We are chained because we are wild animals and mustn't leave our enclosures. Otherwise, the people who pay to come to the zoo would have nothing to gawk at."

"So, you are captives?" Poppy asked.

One of the other elephants answered, "Captives? You could call it that, I suppose. But where exactly would we go if we were to escape? Honestly, it's all a bit silly."

"A bit silly, but we have a job to do," Gemma said a bit forlornly.

"A job?" Niles asked.

"Yes, our job is to be ourselves as best we can under the circumstances. People come simply to watch us every day, and while I am impatient at times, their interests are pure for the most part. They ooh and they ah and are fascinated by how different we are from them, yet the strangest of ironies is they so often fail to see that it is our similarities that make it all really fascinating. We study them too, you see! It is what one might describe as a mutually beneficial relationship." All three elephants laughed and snorted.

"So," Gemma added, "we are here for you to observe. To entertain you and fascinate you. But, honestly, it is late now, my small friends, and old Gemma is tired, as are my two dear girlfriends here."

"Well, we were just going.," Niles said cheerfully, although truthfully, he felt rather sad.

"Follow the path," Gemma called after them, "you will meet some interesting creatures."

"Yes, okay! We will," Niles answered.

"And thank you ladies for your time," Nathaniel giggled as he responded.

Niles and Nathaniel continued along the same path that had brought them to the elephants while Poppy flew on ahead. The evening was warm with a brisk hot wind that blew off the desert. None of them much cared for this seasonal wind, as it played tricks with the normal course of finding one's way around by scent, and for Poppy, it either meant battling a nearly impossible headwind or—when it favored her trajectory—often overshooting her target landing zone. Niles's long hair blew in the wind, and Nathaniel periodically sneezed.

"The ladies back there made me feel sad," Niles remarked as he and Nathaniel strolled.

"Why? They seemed happy enough." Nathaniel stopped and looked at his friend.

"Well, it's sad that their world is so small. I mean, my world was small, but look at me now and how much I have seen and done since I left home. I'm learning what it means to really live, right? And they won't learn what I have learned. Those great creatures will only know that small world. I don't know, Nathaniel. Just makes me sad."

Just as Nathaniel was about to respond, Poppy landed between the two of them. "There is a creature just over there," she said, indicating the path with her wing, "that I think we should talk to. He or maybe she—I'm not sure—is sitting like a human with his back to a tree, wide awake, and . . . I don't know. It looks like he's daydreaming. He's a large one with hands like a human but covered with silver and black fur and has sort of serious-looking face. Anyway, he or she looks smart, and I think we should talk with him or her or I don't know. Just follow me."

Niles remembered Deheune's words, *"sit at the feet of the great silverback"* and wondered if this was who he was supposed to encounter. Niles and Nathaniel anxiously followed Poppy down the path until they came to a two-tiered structure that looked out on an enclosure with a collection of trees in the center. As they walked toward the enclosure, they strode along the lower tier. From this vantage point, they could easily see into the enclosure, as the front was made entirely of glass.

Niles hopped up on a small ledge so that he was standing at the ground level of the enclosure, just on the other side of the glass. Not more than a few feet away sat a magnificent creature, just as Poppy had described, leaning up against a simulated tree and looking wistfully at the sky. The creature briefly turned his head, barely seeming to notice the three of them. Then he lazily turned it back as if momentarily distracted from his musings. All the while, they watched him. His great lips moved ever so slightly, as if he were whispering something to himself.

Nathaniel and Poppy were becoming increasingly impatient and suggested that Niles should say something. But Niles refused, saying that the creature appeared to be busy with something and shouldn't be interrupted.

Somewhat irritated, Poppy said, "Since when have you been one to hold your tongue?" and immediately regretted it.

Niles turned around and looked at her. Sensing her regret, he just laughed and shook his head to indicate his understanding. Niles insisted that they wait until the creature indicated interest in a conversation with them before they spoke. Soon, both Nathaniel and Poppy had fallen asleep while Niles continued to wait and watch the great creature.

"It's such a beautiful night, don't you think?" the creature said in a soothing base tone that was somewhat difficult to hear behind the glass.

Niles was unclear whether the creature was speaking to him or someone else until the creature turned toward Niles and repeated, "Don't you think?"

"Yes. . . ." Niles laughed nervously. "Yes, I do think it is a beautiful night." Niles then coughed a few times but did his best to stifle it in order to avoid calling attention to his condition.

The creature leaned forward on his hands and slowly came to a standing position much as a human would stand. Then he leaned forward and half-walked, half-shuffled on his legs and knuckles closer to the glass where he came so very close that only inches and a sheet of glass separated him and Niles. Niles was frightened by the sheer size of the creature's head, his massive, flared nostrils, his deep-set eyes, and the downturned corners of his mouth, which conveyed a profound sense of displeasure. In spite of his proximity to Niles's diminutive frame, he summoned his courage and stood still. The creature then turned around leaning his back up against the glass and slid down into a seated position, one foot planted firmly on the ground, his knee in the air and one arm resting on that knee. He leaned his head back toward the glass turning it only slightly and spoke to Niles.

"I know you are a curious dog with many questions, and I am here," the creature said. "So, speak, ask . . . if you wish."

A smile spread across Niles's face, and he began: "My name is Niles, and I have learned that we do not live forever. . . ."

As Niles spoke, the creature patiently nodded to indicate his understanding of Nile's story. As the creature listened, he considered whether what Niles sought was confirmation of his chosen course or whether he was genuinely interested in what he had to offer. No matter, the creature thought. He would speak the truth as he understood it. So, when the conversation inevitably turned to the smallness of the creature's world and how it was that he could understand or appreciate what it really meant to live. . . .

The great creature grew quiet again and traced his fingers in the dirt by his side. He appeared again to be mumbling something to himself.

"What's that?" Niles asked and pushed closer to the glass. "I can't hear what you are saying."

"Oh!" The creature leaned his back and side against the glass. "I was just thinking again what a beautiful evening this is. The wind has cleared the skies so you can see the stars so clearly. Do you ever watch the evening sky, Niles?" Before Niles could answer, the creature continued. "So many stars. More than one could possibly count, don't you think?"

"I suppose." Niles was feeling impatient and wanted to continue their discussion.

"Sometimes, Niles, when the winds chase the clouds away, I go wandering among the stars to admire their beauty as if they were diamonds flung against the black skies. I do that without ever leaving this enclosure. Can you imagine such a thing?"

The creature turned his massive head to gauge Niles's reaction and whether the dog was listening. Niles nodded his head up and down enthusiastically to make sure the creature knew he was listening carefully.

"Each day, so many people come to view all of the creatures in this place," said the creature. "I see children, their parents, lonely people, happy people, angry people, sad people. I have my own family who are sleeping now, as we speak. . . . Did you know that Niles? My own family who are always on my mind and in my heart. Niles, my world isn't small. My world is infinite because it is not bound by the limitations of experiencing *this* new thing or hearing *this* new idea or listening to *this* creature's advice." Each time he said 'this,' he pushed one of his great black fingers into the dusty ground beside him. "You see, Niles, our hearts, too, are perceptive organs, capable of seeing what our eyes cannot, hearing what our ears have never imagined, understanding what our minds cannot fathom. My world is anything but small and only grows more infinite (if such a thing were possible) with every breath I take. My world is as big as my imagination is vast."

He laughed, and his laughter was rich and warm and generous.

"And death?" he continued. "Are there things I must learn—things I must do because I am running out of time? Is it the number of wise souls I encounter that will teach me how to really live? If that were true, I should be frantically pursuing one wise soul after another, one more learning experience after another. How many wise souls will I need to meet before I know how to live?" He laughed that luxurious, and gentle laugh once again. "I wonder if you may have observed that for every new thing you add to your basket of experience, you quickly come to see that what you hoped it would give you, it didn't. Isn't one of life's first lessons to learn that our hoped-for expectations are rarely met by what materializes? *Not this*, Niles. *Not this*."

The creature turned his head all the way around to look at Niles and raised his brows as if to question whether he had been understood. Niles was pensive and whispered, "Oh yeah. That's right," which the creature did not hear. Again, Niles wanted to cough but held his breath. HE swallowed again and again to soothe his raw throat.

That the creature didn't hear didn't really matter because he had spoken similar words many times before to others with questions much like those that Niles had asked. And he never knew if the words he offered were of any benefit. He only knew that he believed they were true. And the truth did not depend upon gathering consensus in order to make it true.

*What is true is true*, the creature thought.

The sky was beginning to gradually lighten as evening gave way to dawn.

"It appears that the stars are abandoning the skies, doesn't it, Niles?" said the creature.

Niles shrugged, feeling that somehow he had not gotten from the silver and black creature what he had hoped to—that his expectations had been disappointed.

*Not this*, he thought. *Not this.*

Then he coughed gently, cleared his throat, and coughed again. This time harder, until he broke into one of his full-fledged coughing spasms that would only end with that terrible *ack, ack, agghhk.*

"You don't sound well, Niles," said the creature, "and you should now find a place to rest. In fact, maybe it is time for you to go home. You are tired, hungry, and I understand you are disappointed. But you will need to go now, as the zookeepers will be busy bringing us our food and helping clean our enclosures. Please wake your friends and be on your way. But go knowing that I understand what you want. I am who I am. And you are who you are. I am *where* I am. And I cannot change that. But nothing limits or constrains my ability to fully live my life. My thoughts, my heart, my imagination, my soul, Niles. These things shape the life I live. Your restless spirit has led you to the journey you have undertaken. Mine has taken me to the stars. Good night, my friends."

Poppy and Nathaniel were barely awake as Niles hurried them forward. They retraced their steps to the hedges and wrought iron fence where they had entered and once again were on the other side of the fence beyond the hedge and the swaged chain.

## CHAPTER 8

• • •

# Niles Falls III

NILES WONDERED IF the time had come for him to go home. He felt so tired and weak that a soft bed and a good meal sounded very tempting. His loyalties were divided between trying to finish what he had started, his faithful friends, and missing home. In any case, they opted to move in the general direction of returning to the neighborhood where the three of them had met.

Niles sniffed the ground and, finding the scent of something clearly recognizable, followed it down a path leading still deeper into a more remote part of the canyon.

Suddenly, above them came a rustle of wind and the familiar sound of flapping wings. The owl who had attacked them landed very close to Nathaniel who ran as fast as he could to the cover provided by the tall grass.

"Nathaniel, please come out. You are safe. I am so sorry. I will not hurt you"

Nathaniel poked his nose out from the tall grass. "Are you trying to give me a heart attack?" Nathaniel moaned.

"No no, no," the owl laughed. "I'm here to welcome you. And besides, I have lost my taste for . . . um . . . fruit rats. Where have you all been? I have not seen you in days. Have you discovered what you were looking for?"

"Oh, it's a long story, and Niles is feeling ill, so he needs to rest," Poppy explained.

Niles sought out a comfortable place, sniffing and coughing and sniffing some more until he stood before the stump next to the fallen tree where they had begun their journey.

"Hey, I know this place. It's Close Call Canyon," Nathaniel called from the path where he had fallen behind Niles.

"Yeah, I know," Niles answered, looking tired and wheezing as he spoke.

Poppy, who sat on the stump staring at Nathaniel, added cheerily, "Yeah, it's where *you* almost became dinner!"

Niles laughed and started coughing.

Poppy said, "Sorry, Niles."

Nathaniel, wiping a paw across his brow, said, "Don't remind me. That was way too close."

"Well let's stay here. I really need to rest," Niles said, crawling into the hollow at the base of the stump where the grass and feathers were still plentiful. "I really need to. . . ." And before he could finish his thought, Niles was sound asleep.

"Poppy, you go eat, and I'll stay here with Niles," said Nathaniel. "Maybe I'll take a quick look through the garbage cans down the way to find something for Niles and me."

Poppy sat for a moment, puffing herself up into a big fluffy mass, and then flapped her wings a few times as she stood up straight.

"Hmm," she said. "I don't know if we should leave Niles."

"Go eat!" Nathaniel commanded.

She sighed and said, "Okay. Look after him. I'll be back soon." She took off in the direction from which they arrived.

Niles was feverish and slept hard, his breathing labored. The little whistling noise that Niles made when he exhaled unnerved Nathaniel.

All Niles really wanted was to sleep peacefully, but this wasn't to be. His fevered dreams would not allow it. He slept, but he dreamed . . . and such a strange dream it was.

What was this? A path in the woods. The path was clear, but on either side of the path, the forest was thick with trees and shrubs. As he proceeded down the path, it seemed to close behind him, allowing him to proceed in only one direction. If he attempted to stop, he could now see that the encroaching forest would quickly swallow him. Still, as he was forced to walk along the path, it became progressively darker, not because of the trees but because of a fog of sorts.

He gave little consideration to the path, why he was on it, or where it might lead. A path, he thought, is meant to be followed, and he had little choice but to proceed until it became clear that whether he went forward or backward, he would be engulfed by darkness. He was frightened but kept reminding himself that this was only a dream and could in no way hurt him. Soon, he would wake and join his friends to finish their quest. Their journey.

But it all felt so real. And it took only moments for the encroaching forest to meet the oppressive fog, and he knew he was lost and would never find his way out. But again, he told himself, "This is a dream, and dreams need not be feared." So he courageously decided to explore the meaning of this most unusual dream. First, he asked himself *where* he might be.

*Is this a place?* he wondered.

This place was peculiar in the sense that there were no familiar scents or sounds—certainly no familiar landmarks. Indeed, as he considered it, there were no scents or sounds at all. Experience had taught him that every place has a scent or a sound.

"That's odd," he said out loud. But even his words seemed to be absorbed into the mounting, bleak, woolen darkness and were barely discernable.

Settling over him, this oppressive, dark cloud, which made it impossible to see his own paws, restricted his movement to little more than inches at a time. He contemplated his condition as absurd. He had arrived at a place one might call *nowhere.*

*That's it*, he thought. *I am nowhere!*

Where was this "nowhere," he asked himself. It was no . . . where.

*So, if it's not a place, then exactly what is it? It must be a state.*

Yes, that was it. It was more *a state* than a *place.* But the more he tried to determine his condition, the more disorienting it became. The darkness itself seemed to seep inside his skin so that he became undifferentiated from his surroundings. It was all still more absurd; he was, he pondered, becoming a *no one.* He was becoming *no one* in *nowhere.*

Wherever nowhere or no one was, it gobbled up anything that dared to believe it was *something*, turning it into *nothing.* No one, nowhere, nothing. He was no one, who was nowhere, with nothing. He was absolutely alone. Alone to be with himself.

"To what end?" he asked himself.

What was there to glean from this nightmare other than despair? His confidence that this was all only a dream melted in pools of uncertainty. Courage was useless, for it had no object. There *was* no dragon to slay, no one to rescue, nothing he could confront and stand up to. He could not retreat. He listened as an outsider to his internal conversation, over which he had no control. He was literally at odds with himself—with one side mocking the other.

"A quest?" The voice was dismissive. It echoed what Geddes had told him: "I don't think about it, and neither should you. What have you accomplished other than to hurt the creatures you claim to care about? What have you to show for this so-called quest? What was the point of all this?"

The more he thought, the more alone and full of doubt he felt. Now, here he was, on a path that led to nowhere, paralyzed by self-doubt and anxiety and feeling utterly abandoned.

"Ohhh," he cried to no one in particular.

And then, crying again and again, he soon found himself howling. It was a peculiar howl that arose from somewhere deep inside himself that ached.

It was not pain but a sense of longing to know himself and his life in a way he never had before. The desire to know and to understand what he was to do with his life, how he should live the life he was meant to live. He howled because he did not know what else to do. But this howl, this cry, sprang from someplace different. It was an odd and unfamiliar place. Preoccupied with his own anguish, he barely felt something brush his side—something soft and reassuring.

The silver cat with the blue eyes put her face close to his and spoke:

> *"Weary, sick and hopeless,*
> *This quest exacts a toll.*
> *You've lost your precious innocence*
> *But found your priceless soul.*
> *That cry from deep within,*
> *Despairing but sincere,*
> *screams within your soul*
> *but whispered in God's ear."*

Nathaniel watched Niles sleep fitfully but saw that the daylight hours were giving way to dusk, and so he decided he would go out and find food for Niles when he woke. He wandered down the path through the center of Close Call Canyon toward the homes where it seemed, such a long time ago, he had found a half-eaten hamburger for Niles. He would find something just right for his friend, he thought and smiled.

# CHAPTER 9

• • •

# Dognapped!

Niles slowly opened his eyes when he heard the sound of rustling brush and human voices.

"I think it might be dead." It was a young boy's voice.

Niles wanted to protest but felt too weak. Instead, he lifted his head to see two young boys, one with a stick that he held by his side, the other with a brown-colored baseball cap.

"Holy crap! He's alive. Pick him up," said the boy with the stick.

"You think he'll bite?" The one with the cap hesitated as he bent down.

"Are you kidding? Look at him. He's half dead! Pick him up!"

The boy with the stick pushed the end of the stick against Niles's stomach, which caused him to flinch.

"See? He's not going to bite you! Go on! Pick him up!"

The boy with the baseball cap picked up Niles and held him awkwardly in his arms. Even though the boys were strangers, the touch of another made him feel safe.

"Let's take him to your house," said the boy with the stick.

Niles, suddenly aware that the boys intended to take him, lifted his head, alarmed, and looked for Nathaniel and Poppy, who were nowhere to be seen. He made several pitiful calls for them, which the two boys mistook for having mishandled and hurt him.

"Be careful with the dog, stupid!" the boy with the stick said and playfully slapped the other boy on the back of his head. "You gotta be gentle, right?"

The boys headed back down the path in the direction from which they had come.

"I wonder if my mom would let me keep him," said one.

Then the boys walked in silence, pondering this for a while until the boy with the stick reached over and felt around Niles's collar until he found the dog tag Poppy was so fond of.

"He's got a license, so they should be able to find his owner with no problem."

The boy with the cap frowned and complained, "But they must be terrible owners. You can see he's sick. Man, I really want to keep this dog. I think he likes me."

The other boy stopped and let his stick fall to the ground. He reached over, unfastened the dog collar, and tossed it off the path, saying, "You want him? There. He's yours now."

They both laughed and resumed their way down the path toward the residential area where they continued down the street.

Nathaniel dragged a small sandwich bag with a half-eaten sandwich back to the stump where he had left Niles.

"I got something for you, buddy," he said, looking in the hollowed out stump. He dropped the bag and called out, "Niles! Hey, buddy! Where are you?"

He thought maybe Niles had just gone to take a pee, but then reasoned Niles was way too sick to have wandered out of the immediate area. He called again and again, running up and down the trail.

*Where is Poppy?* he thought. *She'll be able to spot him during a flyover. Where is she?!*

He felt angry, frustrated, and worried.

"Poppy! Poppy!" he called over and over, but no answer . . . nothing.

He sat down outside the hollowed-out, old stump to think it over.

*He was too ill to go anywhere,* he thought. *Besides that, Niles would never leave his friends.*

The boy with the brown cap called for his mother the moment he walked in the door.

"Mom, Mom! You gotta see this. We found this dog up in the canyon. We think he's sick. Can we take care of and keep him? He doesn't have a home." He held Niles up so his mother could see. "No license! I checked. Can we keep him?"

The boy's mother said something about taking him to the veterinarian, adding that she wasn't sure about keeping him. Then, "He's a Yorkie, isn't he?"

"I don't know," the two boys said in unison.

"He *is* cute, isn't he?" said the boy. "It is a he isn't it?" The boy held Niles up again this time letting his back legs drop.

"He's a boy," she said.

Niles was not so sick that he was immune to the humiliation of this whole experience and decided he would wait for the opportune moment, then flee. But the boy wouldn't let him go, and within minutes, they were in the car on their way to the vet.

At the vet, Niles was poked and prodded and squeezed and given several injections.

"I believe he has a respiratory infection, which can be dangerous for an older dog," the vet explained.

"Older?" asked the boy's mother.

The vet told her that Niles was an older dog and that sometimes people who want a younger dog will abandon their old pets. The woman shook her head in disgust.

"People like that should never be allowed to have a dog!" she huffed, then added, "Well, we'll take care of him."

The boy with the brown cap protested that it was *his* dog because he found it. His mother said that owning a dog was a big responsibility, and since this dog had already been abused, it would need the support of the entire family. So, it was settled, she said. The dog would become their family dog.

"He's going to need a name," she said.

"How about Buddy?" the boy answered enthusiastically. "Because I know he'll be my friend. I mean, we saved his life, right?" They all laughed.

Then a young woman who had helped the vet gave them a blue collar, which they fastened around his neck and told them they had given Buddy a rabies vaccine and they should be sure to get him a dog license. They next attached a leash to the collar, and the mother said, "I'll walk him out." Then she added, "We'll have to let his hair grow out so that we can tie it up with a cute little bow . . . blue, of course, and he'll look like a proper Yorkie." She placed Niles the ground, and she yanked on the leash and said, "Let's go home, Buddy."

Sitting in the car on the boy's lap, Niles looked out the window, wondering where his friends were.

Nathaniel waited what seemed like a long while for Poppy's return. Every few minutes, he'd walk up and down the path, calling Niles's name, then muttering something to himself about how he shouldn't have left Niles alone. Poppy finally returned late in the afternoon, and Nathaniel scolded her for taking so long to return.

"You told me to go and eat. I *wanted* to stay with Niles," she protested.

"I know. I know." Nathaniel shook his head. "I'm sorry. I'm just worried."

"I know you are, but I am too!" She decided it was her turn to scold *him* now, then restrained herself for being petty. "Let me have a look around. I'll be back soon."

"Soon? Are you sure?!" he shouted to her as she flew off.

Poppy flew in wider and wider circles above their encampment, searching for any sign of Niles, but she found nothing. Nathaniel marched up and down the paths of Close Call Canyon arguing with himself about the impossibility of Niles suddenly getting up and leaving. It wasn't long before it was dusk, and they would have to settle for the evening because it would be impossible to see now that darkness had fallen. When they got back to the stump where they would sleep that evening, a voice called to them from the darkness just beyond the encampment.

"Who is that?" Nathaniel asked, startled by the sound of someone calling him by name.

"It's me!"

A pair of big, yellow eyes shone in the darkness above. A moment later, Martin flew from a branch and sat to the top of the stump before them.

"I came as soon as I heard." There was a sense of urgency in Martin's voice and demeanor.

"Heard what?" Nathaniel asked.

"About Niles! What do you think?" Martin answered.

"But . . . how did you find out?"

"Hmm . . . heh, heh, heh."

The unmistakable sound of their friend's voice drew their attention to the darkness behind them. Spinning around to see him slowly walking into their line of sight, then leaning on his walking stick they cried in unison, "Leach!"

Leach smiled his big, toothy grin. "It seemed to me that we needed . . . heh, heh . . . a new set of eyes . . . heh, heh. Night vision and all, you know. Heh, heh. Glad to have you here, Martin.

"Listen, I can see just fine and don't want to wait until daylight to find Niles," Martin explained. "Who knows how far away he might travel if we wait. So, you rest while I sweep the area and look for any sign of Niles."

*Of course*, Nathaniel thought. *Night vision.*

It was Martin's night vision that had nearly cost Nathaniel his life. Martin flapped his great wings and was far above them and out of sight in just a few moments.

Leach slowly walked over to stand before Poppy and Nathaniel. "I'm afraid this adventure . . . this . . . heh, heh, *quest* as you say, has just gotten a little more complicated, my friends."

Niles was feeling much better after his visit to see the veterinarian although he was exhausted by the constant attention his new family was giving him. Each one of them took turns holding him on their lap, and while they were nice enough, Niles felt awkward because he didn't know these humans, and clearly, they thought he was someone else because they kept calling him Buddy. The Mama of this house brushed Niles interminably as she spoke of how cute he would soon be when his hair grew out. She gathered up the hair on top of his head, which fell over his eyes, and tied a blue bow around it.

"There!" she said cheerfully, pleased with herself. "Now you can see!"

When the hour grew late, the MAN said that the boy and his sister could take turns having Buddy spend the night in their room. And, so picking him up, the boy took Niles into his room, closed the door, and insisted that Niles fetch a rope that had been tied into a knot, which he threw from one end of the bedroom to the other, urging Niles to have fun with him.

"C'mon Buddy! Go get it. C'mon boy!"

Niles looked at the boy and then the rope and decided he had little interest in playing with the boy. He wanted to know where Nathaniel and Poppy were and how they would find him.

"C'mon Buddy!" the boy called enthusiastically.

Niles looked away when suddenly, he was struck on the side of the head. He yelped, both startled and stunned for a moment. Niles saw that the boy's jaw was clenched and his mouth turned down at the corners in an angry scowl. The knotted rope sat on the ground in front of Niles.

"You better listen to me when I tell you to do something, Buddy! I saved your life, and don't you forget it!" The boy spoke quietly but with an intensity that was both menacing and frightening.

Niles lay down with the knotted rope next to him, just hoping the boy would now go to bed. Instead, the boy cheerfully told Niles they could play catch tomorrow, but now it was time to go to bed.

"C'mon, Buddy." The boy leaned over and picked up Niles, who cringed, not knowing the boy's intentions. Much to his surprise, the boy placed him gently on his bed while he went to brush his teeth and attend to the before-bed rituals. Finally, the boy climbed into bed, grabbing Niles and placing an arm over him as he lay back on his pillow and finally fell asleep.

As he lay under the boy's arm, he listened to the rhythm of his breathing and wondered if it was safe to wriggle out from under the arm's oppressive weight. After waiting for what seemed a long time, he slowly backed out from underneath the boy's arm, surveying the room for any potential escape routes. There were none, of course, and so Niles jumped off the bed and found a spot on the carpet in front of the closet. He scratched the spot a few times and then turned like a corkscrew before settling into this spot for sleep. He curled up in a tight ball, tucking his nose in between his back paws, and wondered where his friends were, how MAN and Mama were.

He thought about how lonely he felt, but he also recalled the words that the great silverback had shared with him about the limitations and constraints we place around our capacity to know how to live, what to do, how to be. Niles recalled how he had said he walked among the stars even while he sat in that enclosure. He also remembered Deheune's words about having found his precious soul. While this made him feel better, he thought, *How can I possibly walk among the stars from here?*

Finally, Niles drifted into sleep.

Martin flew over the canyon and surrounding neighborhood, looking for any sign of Niles, for half the night until he spotted something in the grass along the path that briefly glimmered in the moonlight. He dove for it at full speed, and just before he reached the grassy area next to the path, he stretched his legs with their great talons opened wide and, in the blink of an eye, had the object in his grasp and was again high above the canyon and headed to share his find with the others.

Descending in a flurry of commotion, Martin dropped the object before the others. Nathaniel gasped, covering his mouth with his paw. Leach nodded his head up and down and scratched his chin. Poppy leaned forward, looking at the object as if in a trance, then started pecking at the metal dog tag on the small leather collar. Each of them knew the collar belonged to Niles, but no one spoke. Nathaniel's thoughts went to the worst of all scenarios, Leach was formulating the questions he would ask himself to determine his next move, and Martin was contemplating whether he would take a few more passes over the area before dawn.

Poppy, who had been pecking at the dog tag, stopped suddenly and said, "Well, Niles could not have taken off his own collar. . . . And certainly no creature but a human could have removed it."

"Yes. I think we know this," Leach said. He sat back on his haunches and holding his right paw up as if to underscore his point. "We know it was a human because the collar was removed carefully. You see, it's perfectly intact! This is to say…heh…heh it was not gnawed off." Leach picked up the collar with his two front paws, showing each of them. "And, there is no reason to believe that Niles's human family found him, for they would not have removed his collar." Leach leaned forward and looked carefully at each of them. First Martin, then Poppy, then Nathaniel. "We know, too, that he was not well enough to walk off on his own."

Everyone nodded.

"I fear," Leach continued, "that Niles has been kidnapped . . . er—dog-napped. Heh, heh."

"This isn't funny, Mr. Leach!" Poppy complained.

"I hardly think it's funny, Poppy. Heh . . . heh."

"There you go laughing again," she said accusingly.

"My dear Poppy . . . heh . . . heh. I have not the slightest idea what you are talking about."

"Forget it, Poppy!" Nathaniel frowned. "We need to find Niles, not argue".

Niles slept fitfully that evening, uncomfortable with the unfamiliar surroundings. The sound of the boy's cadenced breathing was a comfort because it assured Niles that the boy was asleep. He was troubled by the boy's unpredictable behavior and knew he would need to be on his guard and careful to not offend the boy again.

Niles's worries went from one thing to the next, which would not allow any sleep. He worried about Nathaniel and Poppy, about MAN and Mama, about whether he had done the wrong thing by leaving with Nathaniel to begin with, and finally, he worried about whether he would ever be able to leave this new home that didn't at all feel like a home. At some point, he must have drifted off to sleep because he found himself face to face with Deheune and her brilliant blue eyes. She was in the boy's room and sat erect, her tail winding this way and that as if possessing a mind of its own.

Niles sat and looked at Deheune, who said nothing. He could still hear the boy's breathing and so was confused as to whether this was a dream or not, but he did not speak. Then came the soft purr and melodic words that could not be words, for the cat was not speaking. Nevertheless, Niles heard these words and understood that they were clearly intended for him.

*"You believe you're alone, but you'd be mistaken.*
*The road you are on, the quest undertaken,*
*Immovable obstacles seem placed in your way.*
*Ne'er turnaround now; to learn, you must stay.*
*Remember my words, or the truth you shall miss,*
*The life that you seek is not this, not this."*

Niles wanted to ask the cat to explain, but found he could not will himself to do so.

*What does she mean?* he wondered as he watched her great blue eyes slowly close and open again, her mouth conveying the hint of a smile.

Jolted from his sleep, the boy had picked Niles up and was carrying him downstairs in his arms as one would cradle a baby. The smell of sausages drifted from the kitchen into the hall.

"Look who I have," he called toward the kitchen.

The boy's father, dressed in shorts, a T-shirt, and sandals, was cooking breakfast. "Put Buddy down, Miles," he said.

The boy did, and Niles thought, *Miles. Miles and Niles!*

The boy's sister, who Niles had learned was called Heather, said, "Remember that Buddy stays in my room tonight."

"Yeah, but I can already tell he likes me best," boasted Miles.

Meanwhile, their mother joined them in the kitchen wearing a pair of fashionable jeans and a paisley blouse.

"Where are you going all fancied up like that?" the father asked.

"Shopping!" Then she held up and let unravel a new rhinestone-studded red leash. "And I'm taking Buddy with me. He's going to the groomer, and I'll pick him up after my luncheon."

Niles looked at each of them as they spoke and did not quite catch the drift of the conversation except that he might be going somewhere.

"I'm giving Buddy the rest of my sausage," Heather announced. "I don't want it."

Niles had been watching the fork with the sausage move from Heather's plate to her mouth and back to her plate again. He was starving. And just as she moved to put the plate down next to Niles, the girl's mother snatched up Niles and attached the glittering new leash to his collar.

"We've got to go or we'll be late. Gotta be at the groomer's by 8:30. Bye," she called as she headed out the door, Niles under her arm.

Niles was very disappointed about missing the sausage.

The groomer was instructed to bathe Niles but not to cut his hair. They wanted him to wear his hair long like the Yorkie show dogs, but to grow his hair floor-length would take months, so for the time being, he looked clean although unkempt except for the blue barrette that kept the hair on his head out of his eyes.

That evening, Niles was exhausted. It seemed everyone in this family wanted Niles to be their personal pet, so he was always being picked up and whisked away to one of the children's bedrooms or taken out shopping or held in someone's lap or being taught how to sit or taken for a walk. What he really wanted was to be with his friends and go home. He alternated between Miles and Heather's bedrooms, but he definitely preferred staying with Heather. Miles was so . . . well, needy. He seemed desperately in need of a friend, which Niles found stifling. Niles considered this and thought he knew something about friendship and wished he could share it with this boy.

In the evenings, after everyone had fallen asleep, was when Niles felt most alone. He would think about his friends—Nathaniel, Poppy, Leach, and Bela—and what he learned about friendship from them. He thought about MAN and Mama and the very special friendship that existed between them. Friendship, he supposed, was not something you could compel another to offer. No, friendship had to be freely given. Something you *give* to another, he thought. Like a gift. The longer he pondered this, the more convinced he became that friendship was a gift. He liked this because it made him feel as if he had something that truly belonged to him but that he could share if he wanted to.

*I wonder if the boy is capable of learning this*, he thought.

As the weeks unfolded, Niles noticed that on school days, Miles came directly home from school to do nothing but stay in his room, play video games, and demand that Niles fetch the knotted rope the boy would throw from one end of his room to the other. Weekends were spent pretty much the same way. Sometimes, the boy would take him for a walk around the neighborhood, but this was no fun at all because the boy was full of commands like sit, stay, and heel that meant nothing to Niles. So the boy would grow impatient with him and yell that he was stupid. Still, the boy seemed to want Niles close to him, even though he would have much preferred to just be left alone.

Niles did become very good at fetching the knotted rope toy, but he despised the game because he feared that if he didn't play the game with Miles, the boy would become angry and speak harshly—maybe even hurt him again.

It had been almost three weeks since Niles had disappeared, and Nathaniel was distraught that his friends were not doing more to find Niles.

"What more can we do?" Martin asked. "I've scoured this entire area day after day and night after night. I haven't seen any sign at all of him."

"Look, Nathaniel, no one's suggesting that we give up!" Poppy said. "C'mon, boy! You have to believe that we'll find him! Okay?" She flew down from where she perched on the stump to be next to Nathaniel. She nuzzled close to him. "C'mon, Nathaniel," she whined.

"Oh, stop it!" Nathaniel pushed her away, and Poppy laughed.

"Ahoy!" Leach's familiar voice was always a welcome one, and Martin, Poppy, and Nathaniel were happy to see him making his way up the trail.

"Good evening, lads and, heh heh . . . lass," Leach grinned as he nodded at Poppy. After greetings were exchanged, Leach spoke. "I think we must recognize the facts. Niles is gone!" His tone was solemn and his manner dramatic. Lowering his head, his eyes rose to gaze at each of them. "And so . . . we will have to use . . . heh heh . . . extraordinary means, shall we say, to *liberate* him."

Leach leaned his walking stick against the tree trunk, then rubbed his front paws together as if he were warming them, nodding and grinning at each of them one by one.

"*Liberate* him? Has he been *captured* by someone?" Nathaniel asked.

The others nodded that they, too, found this to be a curious choice of words.

"What's that supposed to mean?" Nathaniel asked.

"Heh, heh," said Leach. "Yes, *liberate* him, old boy . . . *free* the poor lad!"

"So you *are* saying he's being held captive?" Poppy asked.

"In a manner of speaking, yes. Yes, he is being held captive. He is a prisoner, heh heh . . . of misguided love. A not uncommon phenomenon, I'm afraid to say."

"What does that mean, Mr. Leach?" Nathaniel looked at him confused.

Again, Leach, who had a penchant for dramatic flair, spoke softly. "That will become clear soon enough."

"Well, where is he?" Martin asked.

The question seemed to catch Leach by surprise. "Oh! Heh, heh . . . I don't know."

As everyone moaned, Leach wagged a finger at them saying, "Now, now, now. No room for that kind of thinking here. Niles has been abducted by a family who, I believe, do not live far from here. Their guise is they have 'adopted' Niles."

"Adopted him?" Poppy exclaimed incredulously. "How can they adopt him when he already has a family?"

"The collar!" Martin lit up with understanding. "Somebody took his collar off and threw it in the brush to hide the fact that he already had a family. So, who would do such a thing?"

"Somebody who must be pretty lonely," Nathaniel offered.

"And I'll bet they are young because you never see any older humans wandering through this canyon."

"Splendid start, friends!" Leach clapped his paws together, very pleased with their collective insights. "Lonely, young, living somewhere in the vicinity. You know what to do. Heh, heh, heh. Nathaniel, you walk the wires and explore the neighborhood. Poppy, you and your flock can have eyes all over this neighborhood, and Martin, you conduct the night searches."

"Mr. Leach," Poppy spoke up. "Really now, how did you know he had been abducted?"

"Heh, heh. I don't really think it makes any sense, but but I'm happy to tell you that a rather unusual cat spoke to me in a dream. I think I've seen this cat before." Leach's voiced trailed off. "Anyway, off, off, off we go now!" he said as he clapped his paws together.

# CHAPTER 10

• • •

# He Bit Me!

THE ROUTINE OF sleeping with Miles one night and Heather the next was wearisome because Niles never knew where he was supposed to be. Confused enough by where he was supposed to be on any given night, being uncertain of exactly what the children wanted from him only made it worse. He had to be one way for Miles and another for Heather when all he really wanted to be was himself. To further complicate matters, the two children were becoming more and more possessive of Niles, and they were jealous of any attention he gave to anyone but them and them alone.

As was often the case, on this particular evening Niles forgot whose turn it was to have him as their roommate. He was tired, Heather had gone to her room to do her homework, and he followed her up the stairs to her room. Miles turned off the TV downstairs and called, "Buddy, let's go!" Niles was already sleeping soundly in Heather's room, who had finished her homework and was now reading in bed. Partly because she wanted to annoy her brother and partly because she wanted Niles to stay with her, she grabbed Niles from the end of her bed.

"Quick! Get in here, Buddy," she said as she lifted her bed covers and pushed him way under.

Niles knew that Miles would not think this joke very funny, but, the truth was, he wanted to stay with Heather instead of having to chase that silly knotted rope from one end of the room to the other.

"Buddy, Buddy!" Miles called from his bedroom. "Get *over* here right now!"

Miles's tone became more impatient, leading his father, who was checking on the children, to remind him to be patient and use the right tone with

Buddy so as not to scare him. Miles returned to his own room for a few minutes to seethe. Angry now, he walked into Heather's room without knocking and turned on the light.

"What are you doing, you jerk?!" Heather complained. "Get out!"

"Where's Buddy?" Miles demanded.

"I don't know. You should have been paying attention instead of watching TV. Now *get out!*" She yelled.

The volume with which she yelled caused Niles to jump, which, unfortunately, Miles saw.

"What is that?" He pointed an accusing finger at the lump in her covers toward the foot of the bed.

"Oh, that's nothing," she said and smiled.

Miles hit the lump hard, and Niles yelped and emerged at the top of Heather's bed.

"Geez, Miles!" said Heather, her face screwed up into a sneer. "What are you trying to do? Hurt the dog? Maybe Buddy just doesn't like you!"

"He likes me just fine," Miles said as he picked Niles up.

"Shut my door!" she yelled as he left, but it was too late.

The two of them entered Miles's room, and Miles slammed the door and set Niles down on the floor. He looked at Niles and got down on his knees so he could be closer.

"You like me, right Buddy?" he said.

Niles, of course, remained silent.

"I know you like me, Buddy."

He patted Niles on the head hard enough so that it hurt somewhat. Then he hit him hard on the head, causing Niles to cry out again. Niles ran under the boy's bed, looking for a safe place away from the boy. The boy moved his bed, but Niles remained under it, right in the middle, so the boy could not reach him.

"I'll get you out of there all right!" The boy's voice frightened Niles, who watched his shoes move about the room. "This should do the trick!" the boy laughed.

Then suddenly, the boy was wildly sweeping the baseball bat under the bed to clear Niles out from underneath. When Niles got within arm's reach,

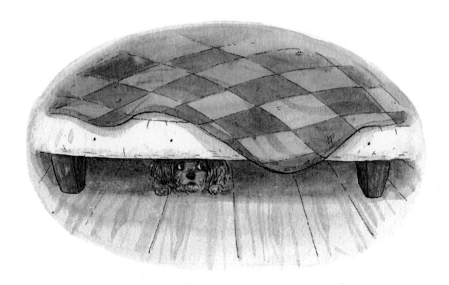

the boy grabbed him by the scruff of the neck, picking him off the ground and causing him to twist and turn and cry out.

"Hey, what's going on up there!" the boy's father yelled from downstairs.

Miles grabbed Niles again. This time by one of his back legs. Niles panicked, reached around, and chomped down on the boy's hand, causing him to squeal and then cry.

In moments, the door was flung open by the boy's father, with the mother and sister in pajamas behind him.

"*He bit me!*" the boy cried.

"Let me see." The boy's mother rushed past her husband and took Miles's hand in hers. "He's bleeding. Buddy broke the skin!"

"Come with me." She took her son by the hand and led him to the bathroom, half talking to Miles, half talking to herself. "You know, a dog that bites once is a dog that will bite again!" Then, in the bathroom, taking her son's hand in her own she asked, "What happened? What did you do!?"

Miles was incredulous. "What did *I* do? *I* did nothing. I just wanted us to play, and suddenly, out of nowhere, he bites me! I can't believe that dog . . . and after we rescued him and saved his life!" Miles's eyes welled with tears.

"Where is Buddy?" The father was scanning the boy's bedroom for some sign of the dog.

Heather looked under the bed and said, "He's under here. He looks scared!"

"I don't care if he's scared," her father said impatiently. "We just aren't going to have a dog that bites in this house!"

Niles cowered under the bed and was visibly trembling. As soon as Niles had bitten the boy, he'd regretted it. He hadn't meant to hurt him. He hadn't considered biting the boy; it had been purely instinctual. He had been frightened and simply wanted to protect himself.

Under the bed, he saw Heather's face appear at the far end and hoped maybe she'd take him to her room. But he also heard her father, his voice gruff and angry, and once again, he feared for his safety.

They moved the bed this way and that, and as they did, he adjusted his position so they couldn't capture him. Then he heard the father say, "This will get him out of there," and he saw the baseball bat again make a sweep that just barely missed him. Then again, and this time, he moved to the furthest point from the bat sweeping the floor under the bed and felt a pair of leather-gloved hands grab him. It was Heather, so he thought he might be safe, but her father took hold of Niles tightly by the scruff of the neck and told Heather to get his leash.

The father tied the leash to one of the posts on the backyard deck and attached Niles to the leash.

"I'm afraid you're out here for the night Buddy, old boy," said the father. "Afraid you may have a little too much spunk for *this* family."

Niles sat, tied to the porch. As the father walked back in, Niles caught part of what he was saying to the family: "The animal shelter . . . tomorrow . . . good home . . . biting dogs . . . euthanasia."

Niles couldn't make out everything he said, but he didn't like the sound of it. Suddenly, he felt tired. Very tired. And he lay down, feeling very sad that everyone seemed so unhappy with him. He thought again about how much he missed his friends and the family where he belonged. As the lights went out one by one, Niles's eyelids grew heavy, and he knew soon he would be asleep.

Just as he was about to lose the battle to sleep, the back door opened, and Miles stepped out in his pajamas. Niles began to tremble and looked for someplace he could hide. Instead, he just took off but reached the end of his leash very quickly and fell backward with a jolt.

The boy sat on the doorstep in front of Niles, hanging his head, looking ashamed. The boy looked then at Niles and again at the porch steps.

"I'm so sorry for this, Buddy," he said. "I know you can't understand this, but when I found you, I thought for sure we'd be best friends."

Niles stopped trembling and sat back now, watching and listening carefully to the boy. The boy continued to hang his head, refusing to look at Niles when he spoke.

"Oh, here," said Miles. "I brought you this." It was the blanket from his bed. "Hope it makes it a bit more comfortable."

The boy fluffed it into a bed for Niles. Then the boy took a deep breath.

"Listen, Buddy. I've never said this to anyone, but the truth is, I haven't got any friends. And it seemed you liked my sister best, and I felt so jealous. I just wanted you to like *me* best."

He hesitated a moment and then looked up, surprised to see Niles looking directly into his eyes.

"I guess you can't force someone to like you right?" said Miles. "Not even a dog."

The boy had water dropping from his eyes—the water Leach had spoken of—and Niles remembered that this meant he was sad.

"Well, I'd better go to bed," said Miles. "I'm really sorry about this and especially that you'll have to sleep out here tonight. My dad says we need to take you to the shelter tomorrow, but I'm going to tell him it was all my fault and that I hope we can keep you. I think . . . well, I *hope* he'll say yes."

Niles cautiously nuzzled close to the boy, who petted him gently. Niles remembered what Bela had told him about others. Try to be kind to all creatures, because they carry a heavy burden. He regretted biting the boy and rather felt compassion for him.

*This boy carries a heavy burden*, he thought.

Niles sniffed the Band-Aid on the hand where he had bitten him, giving it a lick.

"Good night, Buddy."

The boy ruffled the hair on Niles's head, walked inside, and closed the door behind him. Just as he did, the boy's attention was drawn to movement in the tree at the side of the house. It was there and gone all in the blink of an eye—something gray moving along the lower branch there.

"Was that a possum?" the boy asked no one in particular. "Maybe a squirrel."

Niles wondered if it was . . . if it might be . . . Leach, but he decided it would not be wise to get his hopes up only to be disappointed again. He then curled up on the blanket the boy had brought him and promptly fell asleep.

Soon after he'd fallen asleep, the gentle purr of the cat's now familiar voice called him.

*"Niles. Listen, Niles."*

Niles no longer thought to question whether these visitations were dreams, visions, or just hallucinations. What he did feel was that they were real in some way that he apparently could not understand, and because they seemed important, he listened to the cat with the cobalt eyes who, at this moment, sat in the very same place the boy had just a short while ago. Her voice was soothing but authoritative, and Niles listened carefully.

> *"Your work now is done here, but make no mistake;*
> *Lessons were learned, and from them you take*
> *The kernel of truth, a sparkling jewel*
> *That you learned through your journey, unattainable in school.*
> *Your friends on their way now, those who you miss,*
> *To continue this journey just as you wish.*
> *But remember my warning, there will be no bliss.*
> *The life that you seek is not this, not this."*

Niles again wondered if he had been asleep, or had he just encountered, again and again, a cat who might very well be real—a cat offering him what? Guidance? But how could her strange words be construed as guidance unless they spoke of something he simply had no way of understanding?

"Not this, not this," he said aloud.

He wondered about these words. She had spoken them in nearly all of their encounters. It was confusing, but it was almost as if she were telling Niles that in each of his encounters, he had somehow missed the mark.

"Not this, not this," he said again aloud.

*What does that mean?* he wondered.

# CHAPTER 11

• • •

# An Escape Plan

LEACH AMBLED UP the moonlit path through the center of Close Call Canyon and shouted.

"*Oh ho!* The poor boy has been discovered!" Then, mostly talking to himself he added, "And, heh, heh, I barely recognized him with that long hair and little bow atop his head. Heh, heh, heh." He called again, "*Oh ho!* I have found him!"

Nathaniel, who was exhausted from weeks of walking the wires behind people's homes, had been resting in the hollow of the stump, rubbed his eyes and smiled. "Where is he?" he asked.

Poppy, who was perched on a branch above the camp, sleeping with her head turned and beak tucked into the place between her wings, quickly fluttered to the ground close to Leach. "Yes, where is he?"

"Almost under our noses!" explained Leach. "Indeed, you must have passed over the home many times," he said to Poppy. "And you must have sat on the phone wires and fruit trees behind their home over and over," he said and nodded at Nathaniel. "Heh, heh. Funny how these things work." He cocked his head as if to think for a moment, then added, "But no matter now, mates. I know where he is." Then he spoke pensively, adding, "But it is an odd setup." He scowled as he said this then added. "Wait till the others arrive, my friends. Then we must devise a careful but *clever* plan."

Almost as soon as he completed his sentence, Martin and three smaller owls landed in the encampment.

"Well, well . . . who are these fine-looking youngsters?" Leach asked.

Nathaniel slowly backed away, as this was the first time they had met Nathaniel.

Martin puffed himself up with pride and explained, "These are my boys. They're here to help. I'd like you to meet Arthur, Martin Jr., and Bartholomew."

Leach nodded his head approvingly. "Heh, heh, heh. Let's see . . . Artie, Marty, and Bartie! Heh, heh."

Martin and Nathaniel laughed, but the boys stood silent and seemed uneasy. Arthur's attention was fixed like a laser on Nathaniel, who was growing increasingly self-conscious and, frankly, nervous. Finally, Martin took notice and reached behind him, giving him a swift wing-slap on the back of his head and admonished him in a whisper not quite loud enough for all to discern. Arthur turned his head toward his father and complained, "But dad. . . ." Martin's eyes grew very large as he looked sternly at his son, and Arthur's plaintive words trailed off. Leach smiled ever so slightly while Martin winked at Nathaniel. Nathaniel gave him a nervous smile.

Leach clapped his paws together. "Okay, time for us to convene. This is complicated, and we must complete this operation tonight!"

The evening was rather chilly and Niles did his best to nose the blanket into place in order to stay warm. Between short periods of sleep, he woke thinking about the words, "Not this, not this," and wondered what this might mean. Then he'd fall back to sleep.

The gate that closed off the backyard of Miles and Heather's home was no obstacle to Leach or the others executing the agreed upon escape plan. The challenge would be getting Niles out. To do that, they would need to get that gate open. Martin had an idea. He called his boys—Arthur, Martin, and Bartholomew to explain his plan. None of them, he explained, could open the gate on their own.

"Duh, Dad," Arthur whispered, which drew another wing-slap from Martin. "Geez," Arthur said and scowled.

So, since they couldn't open the gate, they would simply have to go *under* it. All three boys looked exasperated with their father's conclusion.

"And how are we going to do that?" Marty asked.

"Well, we need someone who can dig a hole large enough to allow Niles to squeeze under the gate."

The boys smiled at one another, stifling their giggles. Martin looked at his boys, who believed he wasn't aware of their smirks, and heaved a sigh, thinking all this was part of the duties one must endure with fatherhood. But these boys, he thought, were going to learn that their old man was one wise owl this very night.

Leach had pretty much figured that their principal aim was to have Poppy strategically place Niles's collar with the dog tags identifying his owner in a conspicuous place, where the boy's parents would find them. This way, the parents would see that Buddy, or rather, Niles, did indeed have a home to which he should be returned. The collar would have to be discovered by the parents, though. If the boy should find it first, there was no doubt he would attempt to hide it. The backup plan was to have Nathaniel, under cover of darkness, quietly make his way through the yard and gnaw his way through the red, rhinestone-covered leash that bound Niles to the porch. Finally, Martin claimed to be on friendly terms with an agreeable and not-so-very-smart hound down the block whose family always let him out in the unfenced front yard before dawn to do his business. Timing would be crucial.

Martin and his boys sized up the gate to see just how much digging would be required for a hole big enough for Niles.

"This shouldn't be too big of a challenge for . . . oh, what's his name . . . well, the old hound." Martin was walking back and forth before the gate and kept peering under it for some reason, even though the gate was of the chain link variety and one could see through.

Bartholomew asked Martin, "What are you doing, Pop?"

"Hmm? Oh, well, nothing really. Well, no, I'm thinking. I'm thinking you boys are ready to step up, and I want you to go meet the hound, tell him you are my sons, explain what we are trying to accomplish, and get him over here to dig a hole! Can you do that?"

"What's the dog's name?" Martin asked.

"Oh, I can't remember, and it really doesn't matter. He's not very bright but is out in front of the house I showed you every day before dawn."

Martin continued pacing back and forth in front of the gate. The boys looked at one another, and Arthur said, "Sure Pop. We can do it. Can't we, dear brothers?" Arthur nodded his head, indicating yes in an exaggerated fashion, and his brothers followed suit.

"Okay, then," said Martin. "Let's go!"

Marty was first off, then Arthur, followed by Bartholomew.

Meanwhile, Poppy had gone to retrieve Niles's collar from the hollowed-out stump where she kept it hidden. Brushing away the leaves and grass with a strenuous flapping of her wings, she found the collar undisturbed. Poppy thought the silver tags glistening in the moonlight were beautiful and fixed her gaze on them hypnotically, trying to come up with as many descriptive adjectives as she could to capture in words their beauty.

*Silvery, shiny, diamond-like, little mirrors, star-like. . . .*

And so, on she went, seeming to forget about the task she had been assigned.

Nathaniel was positioning himself on the telephone wires that ran through the branches of the tree in the backyard. He could be at Niles's side in a moment. As he watched Niles sleeping in his blanket on the porch all alone, he felt a wave of sadness coupled with utter joy at having found his friend.

Artie, Marty, and Bartie, as Leach had called them, were near the home where their father had told them to expect to find old what's-his-name, the not-very-smart hound. They flew circles around the home, calling, "Here boy, here boy," but with no luck. The three of them were conscious of the time and didn't want to let their father down—or his friend Niles. They perched next to one another on a branch they calculated was right outside the house with the dog their father wanted them to retrieve when Artie whispered to his brothers, "Hey, look."

A silver cat with bright, beautiful blue eyes that they were certain glowed in the pre-dawn darkness strolled by on the ground, aloof and indifferent to the dangers the night might possess for a lone cat. As she passed by the tree in which the brothers were perched, she looked up at them and kept her eyes fixed on theirs as she passed by.

When she finally passed, Bartholomew shuddered and said, "She may be pretty, but she gave me the creeps."

Before his brothers were able to offer their opinion, Marty spied a huge dog slowly walking what must have been just a short distance behind the cat with the strange blue eyes. But the cat now gone had disappeared from their consciousness.

"Okay, boys, this must be our target," Martin whispered, despite the fact that no one had seen the dog exit from the house where they understood he lived.

Arthur whistled to get the dog's attention. When the dog looked up, they could see he was tired. He stared for a moment at the three owls as if trying to make sense of why these three owls would be summoning him.

"Hey, boy. Here, boy!" Martin said enthusiastically.

The dog sighed and spoke. "The name is Snyder, not 'boy.'"

"Sorry," they all offered, shuffling about, appearing to be a bit embarrassed.

"What can I do for you…boys?" The dog was quite large with a dirty, white muzzle and a brown mask that wrapped around his black eyes and ears, which were folded forward. His chest and front and back legs were white, speckled with what appeared to be dirt, and his girth was wrapped with a black belt. He was a sorry sight indeed, and all three of the brothers felt that the owner should have been scolded for doing so little to care for him.

"Our father has sent us to you to ask you a favor." Artie began.

"Sent you to *me*?" Snyder asked, suddenly more alert. "Who is your father?"

"Martin", Bartholomew answered.

"Am I supposed to know who that is?" Snyder scowled at the three owls.

"Yeah, Martin. Anyway, he knows you and sent us to get you. We need your help to dig a hole under a fence."

"Well, I guess that shouldn't be a prob—" Then, stopping short, he turned his head to look up at them and ask, "Just what are you guys up to?"

"Well, it's complicated" Martin continued, "but, in a word or two, we're helping our dad's friend Niles escape from the house just down the street. You see, Niles is a dog, and. . . ."

"What's he want to escape for? What I wouldn't give for a home!" Snyder said.

The brothers looked at one another, confused.

"But don't you have a home, Snyder?" Bartholomew asked.

"Nah. Abandoned down at the beach by a family who wanted a companion while they were on vacation. When vacation was over it was, 'See ya!' Pretty cold, huh?" Then Snyder sat back and, using his right rear leg, began scratching his ear while continuing to speak. I'm . . . up . . . here . . . Oh, oh. Hold on. Oh. *Ahhhh*. That's the spot. . . . Sorry." He stood again. "I'm here because some spooky cat with great blue eyes asked me to follow her here and then, 'poof.' She was gone."

"Oh, so I guess you're the wrong dog," Martin said forlornly.

"Gee, thanks! I've been hearing that my whole life. Wrong dog for this, wrong dog for that. That's why I'm homeless, I guess. I'm just the *wrong dog* for everything!"

"Oh, that's not true. C'mon, now!" Martin said.

"Shut up, Martin", Arthur spoke through his clenched beak.

"*I* can dig a hole, but if you want some other dog to dig it, it's all the same to me. But what's he got that I haven't? Maybe you can get me something to eat if I help. How about it?"

Arthur spoke up. "You'll do just fine. We're glad for your help, Snyder."

Arthur and Bartholomew began slowly flying toward the house where Niles was, and Martin ran and flew alongside Snyder.

"So, what do you think about that blue-eyed cat?" asked Martin. "Huh, Snyder?"

"Well, she was an odd one, all right," Snyder said. He shrugged, then started to run in order to catch up with Arthur and Bartholomew. "C'mon, let's get this show on the road!"

As they neared their destination, the front door of the house they'd been waiting in front of down the street opened, and a not-so-smart hound padded down the steps of the front porch to do his pre-dawn business.

They reached the gate to the home where the three owl brothers found their father waiting for them.

"We have him, Dad, and he promised to help," said Martin.

The dog, head hung low, lifted his eyes to meet those of Martin. Clearly disturbed, Martin looked at his sons with bulging eyes, beak open but speechless. His eyes fixed one at a time on each of his sons, and he shook his head no.

It was Arthur who spoke up. "This is a great dog, Dad. His name is Snyder, and he's a real expert when it comes to digging. Let him show you how good he is. Oh, c'mon, Dad. Just let him help."

Martin turned to Snyder and said, "Just to be clear, you didn't see anything here tonight, okay. Are we clear?"

Snyder smiled, saying, "Hey, no problems from me. I see nothing!" Then, sniffing at the gate for a moment, he turned to Martin and said, "May I?"

Martin nodded, and Snyder began furiously digging a hole under the gate in the chain link fence. He was a pretty good-sized dog, and the task did indeed seem easy. Great clods of grass and dirt flew between his legs, and in no time, there was a sizable pile of earth behind him, as well as a sizable hole under the fence before him.

Meanwhile, the others were enacting the plan, as discussed. Nathaniel had jumped from the wires strung between the telephone poles that ran through the backyards of the neighborhood's homes, and he descended through the branches of a plum tree to the ground. He quietly ran to the porch where Niles was tied to a post at the corner.

"Hey . . . Niles," he whispered as he shook his paw.

As he looked at Niles sleeping, he realized that he would never have recognized him if it hadn't been for Leach's discovery. Niles's hair was quite long now—almost floor length, with the hair on his head tied in a blue ribbon. He shook Niles's paw again.

"Niles . . . buddy. Wake up."

Niles leaped to his feet, ready to fight, yelling, "Hey, watch it!"

"Shh. Easy, Niles. You *must* be quiet. Please!"

"Oh!" A flash of recognition crossed Niles's face. "Nathaniel!"

"Shh. We're gonna get you outta here!" Then Nathaniel looked Niles up and down. "You sure do look...cute . . . for a girl!"

"Oh shut up, Nathaniel," Niles whispered.

"Sit still." Nathaniel looked over the red leather and rhinestone leash to determine where to gnaw through. "I'm going to try to cut through way up here in case you need to run for it," he said, indicating near the collar. "Then, you won't be dragging that ugly thing behind you."

Nathaniel began gnawing on the leather and made good progress. Just as he was about through, Poppy fluttered over their heads carrying Niles's collar in her talons.

"Poppy!" Niles called

"Quiet!" scolded Nathaniel.

Poppy dipped her wings to acknowledge Niles and dropped the collar right in front of the back porch entrance to the house. *Perfect*, she thought.

Nathaniel instructed Niles to strain against the leash, and within moments it snapped, sending Niles tumbling forward.

At the same moment, Snyder completed the hole under the fence gate and was so excited by the breakthrough that he forgot it was intended as an exit. Snyder scrambled under the gate and started running and barking as fast and as loud as he could. Once in the yard, he saw Niles and Nathaniel and began running with all his might directly at them, barking like a fool, his nose covered in dirt and mouth wide open. He looked terrifying, and neither Niles or Nathaniel had any idea why this mad dog was charging after them.

Nathaniel yelled, "Run!" as he took off for the cover provided by a large shrub.

Niles looked at the dog coming toward him in what now seemed to be slow motion, with his ears back and teeth bared. Niles wondered for a fraction of a second why this big dog might want to hurt him, but nothing came to him. Lights were going on in the house—including the back porch light, which only served to better illuminate the charging dog. Niles felt faint.

But then, he remembered what Leach had said. An empty package was of no interest to an attacker.

*Empty, empty, empty*, he thought.

And it was as if he really were empty except for the sound of a song which he heard softly yet distinctly.

*Send your spirit off to wander*
*Among the stars, the skies, and yonder.*

*Wisdom, insight, beauty gained,*
*Our world, our life, our vision aimed*
*Toward higher goals, a greater good*
*For those who, restless, think they could*
*Understand their life's call*
*And how it fits within it all*
*What difference, tell me, will I make*
*To those along the path I take*
*The purest truth is yours to own*
*But known by spirit and it alone.*
*Release and let its seeds be sown*
*But ne'er forget to sing it home*

The charging dog almost upon him, Niles closed his eyes and simply relaxed as his body, folded, and fell into the grass.

There was a scream from the porch. "*Nooo*! Don't!" It was the boy, Miles, in his pajamas watching the dog charge Niles and Niles dropping like a stone.

The dog immediately stopped before Niles, wagging his tail and sniffing him. He whined again and again as he nosed the side of Niles's body to encourage him to get up. The boy ran out into the yard, followed by his father and mother. They stood over Niles. The boy's father picked Niles up, his body limp in his hands.

"What happened!?" the boy cried.

"I don't know," his father replied. "This dog here didn't touch Buddy, yet Buddy seems. . . ." He turned to his wife. "Honey, can you hear a heartbeat?"

He handed the limp dog to his wife who held her ear against Niles's chest. She shook her head.

The boy's crying grew louder. Heather walked up from behind and tapped her father on the back.

"This was by the door," she said and handed her father the collar with the dog tags.

"What is this?" he asked.

"It's a dog collar for a small dog," said Heather.

"It says, 'My Name is Niles. If lost, please call 619-523-3181.' Where did it come from? How did you get it?"

"It was right by the door when I walked out just now," said Heather.

"Is it Buddy's?"

"Let me see," Heather said, approaching her mother who held Niles limp body in her hands.

The collar fit perfectly, and both parents looked toward their crying son. The stray dog was by the boy's side, offering what comfort he could.

# CHAPTER 12

• • •

# The Cat With The Cobalt-Blue Eyes

NILES REMEMBERED FALLING back into grass as soft as Mama's feather comforter. All fear was now gone; there was nothing but a distant hum in the background that wasn't unpleasant—more like a white noise.

He wondered where he was. But it was clear he wasn't really *any*where. There were no distinguishing landmarks, nothing to help him get his bearings. Yet it wasn't uncomfortable, and, in fact, it reminded him of the moments when he'd sat on the bluff and looked out at the sea. It was so beautiful, he remembered. And this barrenness, so tranquil and serene, was sublime. He sensed, indeed he *knew*, he was not alone, and within moments, he heard the voice he had anticipated he would. Soft, feminine, but friendlier than it had been previously it sang gently.

*Send your spirit off to wander*
*Among the stars, the skies, and yonder.*

Then she spoke. "Niles, I see that you have learned a thing or two from that old master, Mr. Leach." Then the cat laughed gently and kindly.

"Is this what it means to let your spirit wander?," asked Niles. As he spoke, he noted that his voice was no longer raspy or hoarse. "Has my spirit wandered away? Taken a walk? Has Niles left Niles?"

"It's only for a short time, but I have been expecting you."

"Oh, really?"

"Yes, the dog . . . did you like the dog? By the way, he is actually very kind. My idea. And he'll make a wonderful pet for that troubled little boy.

"He nearly scared me to death . . . hmm. Literally!"

127

The cat smiled, which put Niles at ease.

"Where am I?" Niles asked as he fixed his attention on the cat.

"Why, nowhere. You are nowhere."

Niles's befuddled expression changed to a broad grin when the cat laughed.

"Now," Deheune said as she studied Niles, "I will share with you a mystery. But remember, mysteries are in themselves unknowable, so you mustn't try to grasp what I am going to tell you as knowledge. But you will see and understand. Only from nowhere can you see everything."

"But. . . ." Niles shook his head, frustrated.

Deheune placed one of her paws to her mouth as she purred, "Shh. Come with me, and you will understand."

They walked for just a short while when Deheune suddenly sat down.

"Now look," she said and appeared to toss something Niles could not see into the air.

Whatever she tossed exploded into a rainbow of colors surrounding them. The colors swirled into shapes, and soon, what had been two dimensional became three dimensional. While they had not moved at all, it appeared they were high above the ground, and for a moment, Niles found himself dizzy and disoriented. The sensation was that they were floating high above a long row of homes with fenced backyards.

"Hey, I know that place! That's my home! And *my* backyard!" he exclaimed, his voice filled with wonder.

Then, as they went still higher, he saw Close Call Canyon, where they had spent so much time over these many weeks.

"I never realized . . . I mean, it's so close to my home!" he said, incredulous, now looking puzzled at Deheune, as if there had been some sort of mistake.

They ascended still higher, and soon Niles saw the park and the woman who had shared some of her lunch with him. Then he saw the sandy beach that stretched on toward the horizon and the gulls calling forlornly to one another. He saw Bela, the one-eyed one-legged gull who had been so kind to him and his friends. He saw the sea and the magnificence of its size, filled with creatures including Shui qi and his friends who playfully jumped and almost seemed to dance on its surface. He saw the house where he lived with his new family, and Miles and Heather, as well as their parents. He saw Nathaniel hiding in the shrubs and Martin, along with his boys, hidden behind the house. He saw Poppy sitting conspicuously on a branch, keeping a careful watch on the events below her. He saw the dog that so frightened him—although from this perspective he appeared harmless.

Finally, he saw himself, lying in the grass still and lifeless.

The cat smiled at Niles, who was busy taking it all in. "What do you see?" she said. "And tell me, now. . . . How will you live the life you were meant to live, Niles?"

"Nothing is as I thought it was," he answered. "I hear your voice and the words, 'Not this. Not this.'"

"Yes," she was listening intently.

"And from here. . . ." He shook his head and looked at the cat, smiled, and said, "Actually, from *nowhere*, I see so much. I see things as if I am looking through the eyes of Nathaniel, of Poppy, Martin, Bela, Shui qi. And what I can see is that *alone*, they are—or, I should say *we* are—unable to see with complete understanding…that insight is a collective endeavor."

Niles considered how different but limited each individual perspective was. Then he murmured to himself, "Not this, not this."

Turning back to Deheune, he continued. "But I also see that 'not this' means . . . well, it means *this* and still more. What I see alone is so limited. It means, '*this* and *this and this and this.*'"

As Niles gazed on everything from *nowhere*, he felt a profound sense of appreciation for the very limited ways all creatures saw with only partial understanding. And yet they were so easily led, by these limited insights, to believe that they understood the truth. He pondered that his concern for *how* he should live his life meant something entirely different from what he had supposed. Living life as a matter of what one should *do* from moment to moment missed the more important matter of how one should *be* in the world.

*Decisions about* how we act *should flow from who we* are, he thought.

"And who are we?" he asked himself.

Looking out over the immensity of everything before him, he thought, *we are simply a small part of something far greater than ourselves.*

"We are so small," he said, laughing. "I mean, I had no idea! How can someone so small believe that they alone can possess the mystery of how we should live?" He paused and whispered, "We are just a small part."

"Small yet not unimportant, Niles," Deheune said authoritatively.

"Important . . . perhaps," Niles answered. "But still just a small part of something so vast, so grand. Important alongside everything else that is important."

He loved this . . . what? This reverie. . . . How wonderful to be part of all this, he thought.

"Grateful...humble" he whispered. "We should live knowing that truth is infinitely more complex than one creature can possess. It is this and this and this. Gratitude and humility. Grateful for the privilege of being part of all this." He lifted his paw in a sweeping motion. "But humble, recognizing that while we may possess the truth, it is really only a small part of it. It is incomplete without others. That's how we should live . . . how we should be."

He smiled at the cat who was staring at him.

"Niles," she whispered. "It is time for you now to go home."

"I know," Niles agreed. He was quiet for a moment, then added, "It is funny how when you encounter the very thing you think you have been looking for, it somehow no longer seems to be what you are looking for. I mean, the moment you discover it, it dissolves. It's like just saying the name of it causes it to dissolve. Not this. Not this." Niles held out and looked at his paw, which he turned upward. He looked at his paw as if it contained something very precious. Then he looked at the cat and said, "Not this, not this," as he turned his paw over as if dropping something he held.

The cat smiled and nodded her head up and down, her blue eyes brimming with excitement and tears.

"And will you be content at home?" she asked.

"I don't know."

The cat kissed Niles on his forehead and said, "Niles, you are a wise old man."

They both laughed.

"Look, he's waking up, I think!" Heather shouted.

I thought we had lost him!" said the children's mother. "Maybe he just fainted!"

"Oh my god! Dogs don't faint, Mom!" Miles corrected his mother.

Niles blinked a few times and found that his eyes needed to adjust to the light. When he did and everything came into focus, he saw that he was on Heather's lap while she sat on the grass. Miles loomed over them with the dog that had frightened Niles at his feet, wagging his tail, mouth open with what Niles thought was a big, stupid but endearing smile. The children's mother also stood over Niles and Heather with a cell phone in her hand.

Heather put Niles down on the grass, and he appeared to all present as if he were just fine, looking keenly at each person's face, wondering what was wrong because, he sensed, something was definitely wrong.

The children's mother wore a serious expression and asked Heather to put the stray dog on a lead since they would need to take it to the animal shelter. There were protests, but she replied, "Just do as I say, please!" Her voice was tense, and the veins in her neck bulged, which Niles took to mean she was in no mood for nonsense.

After Heather took the stray dog to the house, the boy's mother asked Miles if he was the one who had taken the collar off Buddy so that he could claim he was just a homeless dog. It was clear that the boy's mother already knew the answer, so when Miles tried to deny her theory as preposterous, her eyes narrowed, her lips tightened, and she referred to Miles as "young man."

"I want you to be honest with me, young man," she said through clenched teeth.

This seemed to change the trajectory of his argument, and he conceded he had "wanted a dog for *sooo* long" that he may have acted hastily but nevertheless sincerely. Then she squatted down to be close to Miles and said something Niles listened to very carefully.

"Miles, you cannot *make* a dog love you, just as no one can force another to love them." Pointing at Niles, she continued. "This dog has a family. It's only right that we return him. How would you feel? I'm sure Buddy is like a member of the family."

"I know," he whined.

"No, Miles. You don't know."

She took his hand and walked to the far end of the porch so that what she wanted to say would not be overheard.

"Love is *given* not *taken*," Niles heard her saying. "It grows over time as a dog and his family come to trust one another. I don't really think Buddy is the kind of dog that would bite someone without some reason. So, I wonder if there's more to that story that you want to talk about?" She spoke softly to Miles in a tone that indicated the seriousness of her words, but they were delivered without judgment. "A new relationship is very delicate. Kind of like that bean plant we grew in a cup a few years ago—we had to water it and wait patiently for it to be strong enough to survive in our garden, right? We will get you a dog in time because he or she will help you learn how to love. But it has got to be a two-way street—even with a dog! With every relationship, Miles. You must be patient, and you must recognize that you will not always have your way."

Niles made it a point to stay near the two of them, listening to the tone of their conversation, which suggested the boy's mother was a good and wise person. He thought she must be a good teacher, like his teacher, Deheunne, who Niles knew now was gone. He also considered his friends and MAN and Mama and thought, "yes, love is given, not taken."

# CHAPTER 13

• • •

# Mama And Man

THE POSTERS CALLING attention to the lost Yorkie had been up now for some months. MAN and Mama had canvassed the neighborhood handing out colored flyers they had created with a photo of Niles and a promise of a generous reward to anyone who found him. MAN had brought his staple gun, and on each telephone pole they passed, he efficiently posted their flyer with the words, LOST YORKIE: REWARD! After a few short weeks, the posters were weathered and faded, the photo of Niles barely discernible.

Still, they persisted, calling the Humane Society and Animal Control daily but with no luck. The receptionists on the other end of the lines came to know their voices and started calling them by name as they took their daily calls. The receptionists urged them to be patient and, wherever possible, reminded them to remain hopeful.

MAN and Mama spoke to one another about how they missed Niles every evening and even briefly entertained the idea that getting another small dog might lift their spirits, but to do so would be to concede defeat, and they wanted so much to believe that Niles would eventually come home.

Geddes and Tamar had vastly different reactions to Niles's absence. Tamar was sullen and brooded about his absence while Geddes was annoyed and impatient.

"You know what this is, don't you?" Geddes asked Tamar, who was still too young to formulate any opinions on matters of this sort. "This isn't a mid-life crisis. This is a silly old dog on a fool's errand," he grumbled. "You think he's lost? No, ma'am! He is out there '*finding himself*. . . .' Out there seeking some silly notion of meaning and a puppy's idealistic fantasy."

Tamar earnestly asked Geddes, "So, isn't that good?"

"Good? Who knows? I'd say it's just as likely that he is sitting in some cage at the dog pound wondering what went wrong with his search for meaning."

Tamar had heard from Niles many months ago that Geddes himself had been picked up by Animal Control and had spent the night in one of those very same cages.

"So," Tamar asked, feigning confusion. "Didn't that happen to you as well?"

Geddes responded with a weary sigh and blurted out, "Oh, for *god's* sake." And there, the conversation seemed to end.

In the ensuing days, Geddes grew grumpier, and Tamar spent more time surveilling the front yard from the couch in the living room for signs of Niles. On more than one occasion, while Tamar looked out the window into the backyard during the evening hours, she saw a white-faced, grinning old possum on top of the fence that surrounded their property. She dutifully barked at the intruder, who always seemed to make a special point of stopping, acknowledging Tamar, and smiling before he moved on. There, too, were the rat and the parrot, but such creatures were not uncommon, so the barking was merely an obligation, and she paid them little heed.

It was a Saturday fifteen weeks to the day after Niles had disappeared when MAN and Mama heard the phone ring. Because it was a Saturday, neither of them wanted to answer, but MAN picked up the phone just the same.

"Hello. . . ?" said MAN. "I'm sorry—who is this again. . . ? You have what? You have a dog . . . Yorkshire Terrier. You say your son found him? The canyon. . . ? A dog collar. . . . Hmm, but you say it fits—what's that? Yes, yes, of course, we'll come over. And your address. . . . Why, that's just a short walk from here. Yes, uh huh, yes. . . . We're on our way—what's that? He fainted? You think maybe it was a seizure? But he's up and walking around now? We can talk about that when we get there. Okay. Okay. We're on our way."

Mama was watching MAN's expressions as she listened to his side of the conversation, thinking she understood the essence of it. As the conversation ended, she eagerly looked up at MAN as he hung up the phone.

"Well?" she asked.

With a big grin on his face, MAN grabbed hold of Mama's hands, pulling her up from her chair and wrapping his arms around her as he said, "I think we have found Niles!"

Mama smiled and looked at MAN, anticipating his next words.

"I'm not sure what has happened," said MAN, "but something is wrong with him. . . . But she sounded as if she didn't know what she was talking about. Let's just get over there and see exactly what's going on.

# Epilogue

The truth was, Niles had been happy to return home. He laughed when he remembered many of the adventures he and his friends had enjoyed. MAN and Mama were genuinely happy to have him home and greeted him with tears and laughter.

Over the following weeks, routines returned to normal, and there was a sameness about the days that Niles had always found comforting. But, while things *looked* the same as before, for Niles, nothing was the same anymore. He understood things differently, finding meaning—but not necessarily answers—even in ordinary experience, as Deheune had suggested to him. He opted not to attempt to explain to the other dogs where he had been, and he decided not to mention anything at all about the cat, mostly because he knew Geddes would just call him crazy. But he cherished the insights Deheune's guidance had helped him uncover.

The insights were simple, really. He had learned to treasure friendships from Nathaniel, Poppy, and Leach. In an odd way, he had learned that friendship and loyalty were linked. Even when Martin had attacked Nathaniel, Niles had fought him off as a loyal friend. And Poppy and Nathaniel's loyalty to him meant they never given up when he was sick or when he was lost. Friendship and loyalty were indeed precious.

He had learned the importance of generosity and kindness from Bela, who had helped him see that everyone carried a heavy burden, and sometimes, it wasn't very evident. Still, the burdens were there, and understanding others in this manner caused Niles to tread lightly around others, as Bela put it. From Shui qi, he had learned to take nothing for granted—to "wake up," as he had admonished, and see the richness of the world in which he lived. Awareness of the richness of his own world quelled his longing for what he did not possess.

The great but gentle silverback had taught him that joy and contentment could be discovered most anywhere; that they existed as much inside a creature, as outside. If he could find joy and contentment inside, he could see it so much the better outside. From the Silverback he learned the power of imagination; how it could close the distance between him and the stars. He learned that a life that does not go on forever is not such a frightening reality. Perhaps, he pondered, it was the very idea of mortality that urged the spirit in everyone to seek out what their lives would mean.

And lastly, he had discovered that he too had a soul or spirit that dwelled within him and was capable of providing him with the ability to grasp what sometimes seemed beyond understanding. I was his spirit that met Deheunne again and again. It was his spirit that had grasped the meaning of "not this, not this." It was his spirit that had apprehended—but maybe not fully comprehend—that truth was always greater than any particular insight. Perhaps this spirit, he speculated, went on forever. But this, he could not know.

Since returning home, Niles had come to believe that he was living a good life, living the life he was meant to live. For Niles, a good life was about embracing the totality of the life you lived. Living the life you were meant to live was living fully the life you *had*—whether that was in the backyard or flying through the sky or under the sea. Living well did not require you to discover some hidden truth. How to really live—how to live well—was not a secret but evident all around.

He often wondered whether he would have learned all this if he hadn't ventured out, but he would then dismiss the thought with a laugh. He *had* ventured out, and so, that *was* his life. Imagining his life any other way was a pointless exercise because an imagined life simply did not exist. Niles was living well and so, was content knowing this.

He continued to visit with Nathaniel from time to time, who would come by to assist with finding a ripe avocado. For a time after returning home, he and Nathaniel would have long talks in the early evenings after supper. Indeed, many evenings, he and Nathaniel would reminisce, each of them prefacing their recollection with, "Remember when we. . . ." There was laughter and a deep well of good feelings shared between them.

Nathaniel had found a lady companion of late, and his visits were becoming less frequent. Niles missed him, but he understood. Others, too, would visit, for Niles became known as a generous and distinguished Yorkie who was more than happy to discuss weighty matters with other creatures who made their way to his backyard for a conversation under the avocado tree. The flock of wild conures were regular visitors who could be heard chitchatting in the trees. If Niles was in the yard, Poppy always flew to his side to speak, if only briefly. She always affectionately pecked at his dog license before returning to her friends. She told him that the boy, Miles, had gone to animal control several weeks after the incident in the backyard and had adopted Snyder as his own dog. Some evenings, Martin could be heard hooting nearby. Niles tried explaining some of what he had learned to Geddes, who dismissed him as "woo woo."

He hadn't seen Leach since returning home, but Niles knew he would be nearby. He always was. More than once, he heard Mama calling for MAN, pointing a flashlight outside and saying, "Hey, come here! Look at this possum on the fence out front. He's grinning like an old fool."

*He's no fool*, thought Niles. He smiled as he thought about the quirky old possum.

Niles's cough never was fully cured, and, given his age, it should have been no surprise to anyone when, one afternoon, he lay down on the kitchen floor, so tired. He decided he was happy, that learning his life would not go on forever was not really so troubling. He knew that his longing to understand how he should live was evidence itself that he possessed a soul—a spirit, if you wish. And he was confident that now, as he gave up his body, his journey would continue in a different way. He would miss Mama and MAN, his friends, and his brother and sister, but he was tired now, and the silver cat with cobalt blue eyes called him:

> *"Come to me, dear soul.*
> *Come to me, dear friend.*
> *Leave this body behind,*
> *Let your spirit ascend*
> *To a place of peace,*
> *No yearning persists.*
> *Your longing now quenched,*
> *It is this, it is this."*

David L Heaney

# About the Author

DAVID L. HEANEY has spent his career helping individuals and organizations discover and pursue their own special transformational paths. He received a bachelor's degree from State University of New York at Purchase, a master's degree in marriage and family therapy from the University of San Diego, and a master's degree from the Divinity School at Yale University.

Heaney has served as a parish minister, psychotherapist, and instructor with the University of San Diego's Marital and Family Therapy program. His work over the course of nearly twenty years as an Episcopal pastor and family systems therapist has given him great insight into the psychological, spiritual, and social factors that drive individuals, families, and communities. He is cofounder of the Social Assistance Partnership, an entity that assists health and human-service organizations.

Heaney lives with his wife, Lynda, and their three dogs in Durham, North Carolina.


Illustrated by Alexandra Tatu

Originally from Romania, Alexandra studied graphics and illustration at George Enescu University of Arts. She currently lives in Edinburgh, UK.

Made in the USA
San Bernardino, CA
11 November 2017